UGLY HEAVEN

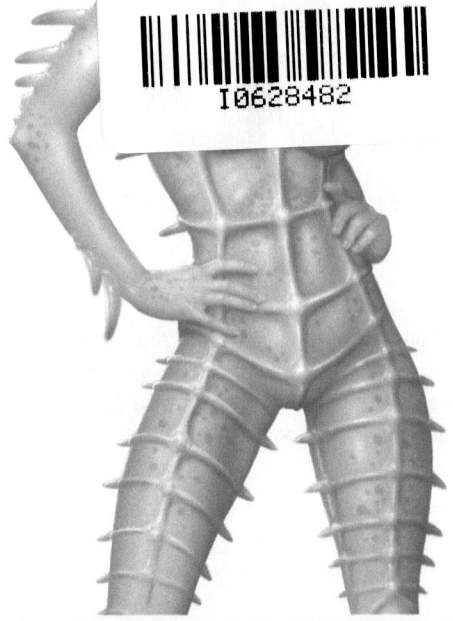

CARLTON MELLICK III

ERASERHEAD PRESS
PORTLAND, OREGON

ERASERHEAD PRESS
205 NE BRYANT
PORTLAND, OR 97211

WWW.ERASERHEADPRESS.COM

ISBN: 1-62105-029-7

Praise for
Carlton Mellick III

"Easily the craziest, weirdest, strangest, funniest, most obscene writer in America."
—*GOTHIC MAGAZINE*

"Carlton Mellick III has the craziest book titles... and the kinkiest fans!"
—CHRISTOPHER MOORE, author of *The Stupidest Angel*

"If you haven't read Mellick you're not nearly perverse enough for the twenty first century."
—JACK KETCHUM, author of *The Girl Next Door*

"Carlton Mellick III is one of bizarro fiction's most talented practitioners, a virtuoso of the surreal, science fictional tale."
—CORY DOCTOROW, author of *Little Brother*

"Bizarre, twisted, and emotionally raw—Carlton Mellick's fiction is the literary equivalent of putting your brain in a blender."
—BRIAN KEENE, author of *The Rising*

"Carlton Mellick III exemplifies the intelligence and wit that lurks between its lurid covers. In a genre where crude titles are an art in themselves, Mellick is a true artist."
—*THE GUARDIAN*

"Just as Pop had Andy Warhol and Dada Tristan Tzara, the bizarro movement has its very own P. T. Barnum-type practitioner. He's the mutton-chopped author of such books as *Electric Jesus Corpse* and *The Menstruating Mall*, the illustrator, editor, and instructor of all things bizarro, and his name is Carlton Mellick III."
—*DETAILS MAGAZINE*

Also by **Carlton Mellick III**

Satan Burger
Electric Jesus Corpse
Sunset With a Beard (stories)
Razor Wire Pubic Hair
Teeth and Tongue Landscape
The Steel Breakfast Era
The Baby Jesus Butt Plug
Fishy-fleshed
The Menstruating Mall
Ocean of Lard (with Kevin L. Donihe)
Punk Land
Sex and Death in Television Town
Sea of the Patchwork Cats
The Haunted Vagina
Cancer-cute (Avant Punk Army Exclusive)
War Slut
Sausagey Santa
Ugly Heaven
Adolf in Wonderland
Ultra Fuckers
Cybernetrix
The Egg Man
Apeshit
The Faggiest Vampire
The Cannibals of Candyland
Warrior Wolf Women of the Wasteland
The Kobold Wizard's Dildo of Enlightenment +2
Zombies and Shit
Crab Town
The Morbidly Obese Ninja
Barbarian Beast Bitches of the Badlands
Fantastic Orgy (stories)
I Knocked Up Satan's Daughter
Armadillo Fists
The Handsome Squirm

AUTHOR'S NOTE

Although I was born Lutheran, I quickly decided against believing in Christianity for one major reason: the concept of Heaven and Hell. Who the hell thought up that crap anyway? Unimaginative parents who were trying to make their children behave?

"If you're really good you get to go to a good place after you die, with sunshine and rainbows and happiness and love and peace and eternal unicorns. But if you're bad you have to go to a bad place after you die, with fire and darkness and devils and scary stuff and ouchies and sadness and you never get to play with toys ever."

And we're supposed to take that shit seriously? What are we in fucking kindergarten or something? Do we also get gold stars on our papers when we're good and have to sit in the fucking corner when we're bad?

Good and evil are too subjective to separate. Christians think gays are evil for being the way they are. Muslim extremists think Americans are evil for being the way they are. I think television commercials are evil for being so goddamned annoying. Murder is evil but it's okay when they call it war. Stealing is evil but it's okay when they call it taxes.

We really don't know the definition of evil. Let's take slavery for example. These days, we think of slavery as nothing but evil right? But back in the days of the bible slavery was such a normal part of daily life that not many thought it was evil at all. Even in the bible the only thing Jesus says against slavery is to try not to beat your slaves too hard.

Thanks, Jesus. You're a big help.

Now imagine what would happen if we no longer ate meat in the future. More and more people become vegan every day. Vegans see eating meat as evil. If one day humans all become vegan and the act of killing animals for meat becomes a crime, we'll all see it as evil in the same way we see slavery or murder as evil today. We'll look back at our ancestors and think they were barbaric and misinformed. Our definition of evil will change. People who eat meat would start going to Hell.

We are not good because we are scared of going to Hell. We instinctually want to be good. We want to be good so that we can be a part of society, because without society survival would be a lot more difficult. It's that survival instinct that keeps us playing nice. This could change if society collapsed. Our survival instincts might start telling us that killing and stealing are okay if they're the only things we can do to survive. So is it evil to do whatever it takes in order to survive? Would everyone start going to Hell until society was rebuilt?

The point is: basing an afterlife on separating good from evil is just ridiculous. We might as well have an afterlife that separates us based on the color of our hair. Or maybe one that separates people who like pickled asparagus from those who don't.

Despite what I think of the concept of Heaven and Hell, I've always had a fascination with the afterlife. It's kind of like having a fascination with outer space. We just don't know what's out there. And though I refuse to believe in Heaven and Hell, I also refuse to believe that there's nothing at all on the other side. That would be just as sad as if we found out we're the only beings in the universe.

As a kid, imagining strange versions of the afterlife was kind of a hobby of mine. I'd play with toys and imagine the characters exploring strange worlds after they died. Sometimes the afterlife worlds would be more like alien planets. Sometimes they'd be like post-apocalyptic versions of Earth. Sometimes they'd be too weird to fully comprehend. But the characters were never immortal in the afterlife. When all of my action figures were killed off in one world they would be reborn in a new one. And the story would continue.

Ugly Heaven is based on one afterlife world I imagined

when I was young. It's a darker version of Heaven, where everything has collapsed into ruin. God is presumed dead and nobody really knows what's going on. The idea of this world stuck with me and eventually I decided to turn it into a story.

I originally wrote Ugly Heaven as a screenplay in college. Then I turned it into prose in 2006, just before I wrote War Slut. It was originally published with the novella Beautiful Hell by Jeffrey Thomas through Delirium Books. My intention was always to turn this into a series, because I loved the world of Heaven and wanted to return to it regularly. Unfortunately, this will not likely happen unless I'm convinced to do so by popular demand. I'd prefer to focus on newer books.

The second book in the series would have been called The Oobleck of Heaven, and it would have been about the three main characters exploring the massive building they believe to be the House of God. Salmon would try to figure out a way to remove his shadow while Tree and Swan try to unravel the mystery behind what happened in Heaven to bring it to its current state. I also have ideas for a third and fourth book: "The Wild Mammoths of Heaven" and "The Topo House of Heaven." If you're interested in these actually getting written feel free to let me know. I might get inspired to come back to this world.

For now, I hope you enjoy this book. It is one of my favorites.

—Carlton Mellick III   5/3/2012 3:35pm

CHAPTER ONE

For some reason, there is a man dangling from a tree limb.

He is fading in and out of consciousness and drooling soda water through various holes on his body, listening to goopy liquids click in and out of his eyeballs. He doesn't know why he is dangling from a tree limb or why such horrible things always happen to him. All he knows is that the unconscious moments are much more pleasant than the conscious ones, so he concentrates as hard as he can to stay as blank as possible...

But, slowly, bits and pieces of the surrounding scenery get caught in his upside-down vision. He tries to block all of everything, grinds his teeth at the effort, but there are things here that are not easily ignored. His eyelids crack open.

What he sees:

A dark green sky clogged with webby clouds. Above the upside-down sky is a stale landscape freckled with murky trees and silver shrubs. Directly below him there are swarthy weed flowers, patches of white mud, and metal wire spiders crawling through red-veined leaves.

The man's mind wakes and wanders. He remembers the sky being a different color from green. He is not sure which color, but it certainly wasn't green. Purple, maybe? White? And trees weren't black and drippy. Or were they? This man is not sure about anything at all. Some things have colors he doesn't even recognize.

He puts his hand over his face to shield his eyes, but... his hand is also the wrong color. It is yellow-tinted. He feels his alien body with black fingernails. Seashell patterns coat his skin—similar to tattoos but embossed into the flesh rather than inked. He is absent of clothes and hair. Only the yellow tinting and seashell patterns cover him. He is also absent of a penis, which is something he is positive he used to have before awakening in the tree.

Hands thrashing against his body, desperately searching for a penis, testicles, vagina, anything. It's got to be on his body somewhere, perhaps he's just forgotten the correct location. He jerks at himself until he drops out of the tree and lands on his skull. An insecty sensation crackles inside of his head, but there is no pain or damage.

His eyes creep the landscape for somebody out to get him. Yellow feet sinking in white mud. Eyes wide and foamy.

There are no signs of life in any direction.

"Where are we?" someone asks.

The yellow man shrieks. He tumbles into the mud and turns to the voice. A short salmon-tinted man is standing only a few steps away from him. He is also hairless, with reptilian patterns instead of clothing and flesh-whips for ears.

"I don't remember where I put my brain this morning," the salmon-tinted one says, knocking on his head. "All blank."

The little man steps to the tar-soggy tree and picks a white fig from a branch. He takes a bite and cringes at the flavor, then converses with the tree, "Have I gone crazy? Is this what craziness is like?"

He takes another bite of fig. Another cringe. Then turns to Yellow. "Do you even speak?"

Yellow looks away from him, eyes glued to the black flowers and white mud, unsure of everything.

Salmon retreats to a human-shaped plank of wood and sits. He opens his mouth around the fig, pauses, then tosses it to the ground.

"I feel panicked," Salmon says. "You know what I mean? Frustrated? Everything's... on the tip of my tongue."

He recovers the fig and blows it clean. "It's like deja vu. You ever get deja vu, Tree?"

Yellow jumps out of the mud. "What did you call me...?"

"You can talk." Salmon nibbles on the fig.

"Tree?" Yellow repeats.

Salmon shrugs. "It's your name isn't it?" squishing the fig between his fingers with a mock-browbeat expression.

The yellow man paces. "Where did you come up with Tree?"

Salmon shrugs, tosses the fruit aside.

"Do I know you?" Yellow asks.

Salmon puts on his thinking face, scratches his chin for a moment, then says, "Maybe not."

"Or did you just call me Tree because I was up in the tree?"

"You were up in the tree?" Salmon asks. "What were you doing up in there?"

"I don't know," the yellow one says.

"You must have fallen out of the sky," Salmon says, fingering zigzags into the mud. "Like me."

Yellow nods in agreement for some reason.

"So you just came up with Tree out of the blue..." Tree says.

"It must've been my subconscious talking," Salmon says.

Then Salmon's eyes light up. "Can your subconscious tell me my name? I think I could really use a name."

The yellow man shrugs.

"I can't consciously tell my subconscious to do anything," Tree says.

Salmon turns the other way, then leaps at Tree. "Quick! What's my name?"

"Salmon," Tree says.

"What kind of a stupid name is that?" Salmon asks.

"Don't ask me. Ask my subconscious."

"I hate that name."

"It tells it like it sees it I guess."

Tree turns and heads toward the black-slime hills in the distance, leaving Salmon standing with lizard-tongues flapping out of his nostrils.

"What's that supposed to mean?" Salmon asks.

Tree waves from the distance.

"Wait for me!"

Salmon plucks an armful of fruit from the fig tree and charges toward the yellow man, dropping half of his harvest along the way.

"You just named me after the color of my skin didn't you?" Salmon asks. "I should've named you Banana."

"You're the one who wanted a name," Tree says, walking barefoot into the alien landscape.

A small green-watered brook trembles with burly pink worms snake-swimming upstream. The faces of Tree and Salmon enter the water's reflection, gaping open-mouthed at the creatures.

"What are they?" Salmon's reflection asks.

Tree's reflection shrugs.

"They look like demonic semen."

Tree's index finger dips into the water, rippling their reflections. Salmon's hand lightning-slaps it away.

"Not in there," Salmon says.

Tree steps away from the creek, scanning the area. When his back is turned, Salmon dips his own hand into the water to poke at the strange fish. One worm swims through his palm, creating an electrical burst as it passes through to the other side. Salmon springs back.

"It entered me." Salmon grips his wrist.

"What?" Tree notices a pink blister forming on Salmon's hand. It makes him smirk.

"What if it's poisonous?" Salmon cries.

The yellow man turns to a silvery tree and finds something out of place. The tree's shadow is not tree-shaped. Instead, its shadow is in the shape of a human being with curly hair and outstretched arms. They aren't matched correctly.

"What is it?"

Tree moves in for a closer examination. He isn't sure about the laws of shadows. Perhaps a tree can have a man-shaped shadow and a man can have a tree-shaped shadow.

"This doesn't make much sense at all," he says, turning around to get Salmon's opinion.

12

The shadow moves.

Salmon sees it twisting behind Tree's head. His mouth widens as it slides up the trunk. A living two-dimensional darkness coiling like a snake.

Before Salmon can say a word, it lunges at his yellow friend. Salmon: "Look out!"

Tree tumbles to the ground, rolls to the side, then scatter-crawls to dodge the pursuing blackness.

More of these shadows emerge from nearby bushes. Dozens of them. All human-shaped, but in varieties. There are crooked old man shadows, fat kid shadows, curvy feminine shadows. But without the people attached to them.

Salmon yelps at the shades, not sure what they can do but positive they want to cause harm. He darts to Tree, then past him. "Run!"

Tree hops to his feet and follows. The shadows trail close behind. They are silent, gliding across the white mud like stingrays.

Salmon jumps over the stream and heads up a blue-grassed knoll. Tree jumps after him but falls short and splashes into the green water. He looks down, balancing himself in the cold wet. Pink worms scurry-swim around his ankles. He turns to see the shadows sailing up to the waterside like pools of ink rolling downhill.

Tree climbs onto land and tumbles into the blue grass. He sits on his naked butt as a shadow crosses the stream after him, rippling on the surface of the water.

A violent splash and Tree crinkles into a fetal ball, but the shadow stops its pursuit. The pink worms are attacking it, slicing through its two-dimensional body. It struggles, then bursts into black particles.

The remaining shadows scuttle around the creek's edge, flowing in and out of each other. They do not enter.

Tree doesn't realize his mouth is hanging open with a millipede tongue squirreling into the air. He lifts himself and scrambles up the hill, catching Salmon at the apex.

"Let's go," Salmon says, pointing across the blue grassland

to a white stronghold in the distance.

Out of the slimy black hills, hundreds of human-shaped shadows spill out into the grassland, facing them like an army.

From a rot-wood balcony, an olive-tinted man with circuitry patterns in his flesh gazes across the blue-hilled landscape. He lifts a brown apple out of his wooly underwear and licks dust from its skin.

Emerging from beyond the hills, Tree and Salmon whimper-run for their lives. The olive man peels the soft fruit with his teeth, sneering at the men as they get closer to the fortress. The horde of shadows ooze after them.

Salmon halts at a large pink worm-infested moat. The liquid boils with them. More worms than water. Tree stumbles into Salmon, glances into the moat, then whips around to see the shades closing in.

"Cross," the olive-tinted man yells.

Salmon gawks at Olive, dog-panting. Then turns to the festering water, and back to Olive again. "You're joking."

"Cross."

Tree touches his toe to the water. It thuds against the surface.

"Glass?" Tree asks.

Both men cautious-step onto the transparent bridge and hurry across. Many shadows follow, but explode upon touching the crude liquid. As the men arrive on the other side, they drop to their knees. Tree rolls onto his back, gasping for breath. Olive appears above them, chewing a bite of apple.

"They fall through glass," says the old man, rolling the apple across the moat. "They aren't made of matter."

Salmon pulls himself to a stump, dropping his head, exhausted.

"What are they?" Tree asks.

"What do you think they are?" responds the olive-tinted man with a wide cartoon smile.

Tree turns to the shadows who rustle about the terrain like cockroaches.

"They are like shadows," Tree says.

Olive nods. He strolls along the waterside, chin to the sky, and speaks as if reading a passage from the Bible: "And God said, let Man possess a dark side so that he may be tested by it. And let man's darkness follow him for every step of his way."

Olive beams on Salmon, who picks purple thorns from a foot. Rubbing his feet-wrinkles, Salmon gawks up at the jitter-fleshed man.

"What are you talking about?" Salmon sneers.

Olive raises an eyebrow.

"What do you think I'm talking about?"

Salmon grumbles and waves the olive man away.

"What is this place?" Tree asks.

"Yeah, where are we?" Salmon asks.

"Where do you think we are?" responds the old man.

"Hey, Tree," Salmon turns away from the olive-tinted man. "Remember when I said you were a horrible conversationalist?"

"No," Tree says.

"Well, this guy is worse," Salmon says.

"I don't remember anything," Tree tells the old man.

"What if you never remember anything?" the man says. "You'll never fully know who you used to be."

"Who I used to be?" Tree asks.

"You were once somebody else," Olive says. "But that person is dead. You have evolved out of him and into somebody new."

Salmon is rolling his whip-like ears around his fingers.

"By the way, have you come up with names for yourselves yet?" the olive man asks.

"Tree," Tree says, pointing to himself.

Then he points to Salmon, "Salmon."

"Good," he says, spitting brown juice at a brick wall. "That makes my job easier. My name is Rowak. My job is to name people. I'm not very good at naming, though. It makes me very happy when people name themselves before they come to me."

The olive-tinted man rubs suction cups along his armpits.

"As I was saying, your memory will be fuzzy for a very long time. Years, perhaps. Eventually, you'll dream of the people you were close to. Then important events. You'll know many aspects of the life you once lived, but most likely you'll never know the person you used to be."

"So we're dead?" Tree asks.

"Obviously," Rowak says.

Tree calms his breath. "Are we in hell?"

Rowak shakes his head.

"Heaven," he says.

Tree blinks his metallic eyelids.

"Welcome to paradise."

CHAPTER TWO

The insides of the fortress are mostly stuffed with hay. There are only a couple small rooms in the back. One where Rowak sleeps. One where Rowak eats.

Both rooms are filled with two things: dolls and furniture. The dolls are in piles on the floor. They are made of plants, paint, hay, and rusty spikes for eyes that follow Tree around the room.

The furniture fills most of the space. It is enormous in size, reaching all the way to the ceiling as if made for giants or extremely obese people. It's made of wood but painted to look like stone.

"Why is the furniture so big?" Salmon asks.

"Much of the furniture in Heaven is this big," Rowak says.

"Why?" Salmon asks.

Rowak smiles at him.

They climb into the bulky chairs and rest their chins on the table, like children at a restaurant.

"So now what?" Tree asks, kicking his dangling feet that cannot reach the floor.

"Now what?" Rowak asks.

"Where do we go from here?"

"Where do you want to go?" Rowak asks.

"I've got so many questions," Tree says.

"Questions?"

"We still don't understand this place," Tree says.

"I told you. You died and are now in Heaven. Now you will start your new life."

"I don't think I believe this is Heaven," Tree says.

"Why not?" Rowak asks.

"Heaven isn't supposed to be this way," Tree says.

17

"Then which way is Heaven supposed to be?"

Tree digs through his memory. He's sure that he once knew exactly what Heaven was like, in perfect detail. But now all of the information in his head is a messy soup. The only word he can find in relation to Heaven is the word paradise.

"A paradise," Tree says. "I don't remember exactly what it's supposed to be like, but it should be a paradise. Not like this."

"What if it was a paradise a long time ago but isn't anymore?" Rowak asks.

"Heaven is supposed to be eternal bliss," Tree says.

"What if this is God's interpretation of eternal bliss?" Rowak says.

"Show me God and I'll believe we're in Heaven."

"What if God doesn't want to see you?" Rowak says.

"Then I won't believe you," Tree says.

He jumps down from his chair and cringes at the salty textures on his feet.

"That's okay," Rowak says. "I don't expect you to believe me. Not many people listen to me at all."

Tree leaves the room. He climbs a ladder to the roof.

"Where are the other people?" Salmon asks Rowak.

"In the cities."

"I want to go to a city," Salmon says.

"I will take you in the morning," Rowak says. "There is a small village not very far."

Tree is out on the rooftop throughout the blackish-blue night and into the green-sky morning. There isn't a rising or setting sun, just a change of sky color.

Staring at his prickly yellow knees, he tries to remember how he died or if he really died at all. He tries to remember things, but nothing of his past can come out of the fuzzy blots that fill his mind. He tries to sleep, to leave the unpleasant consciousness, but it is cold and hairy-ant feelings are crawling inside of him.

He watches the shadows stalking the landscape, attaching themselves to trees and rocks and small bubble-backed mammals.

In the distance, there is an enormous creature stagger-stomping across the landscape. It is like an elephant's skeleton, but made of purple meat and long television antennas. Clawing through the black-slime hills.

"You've been up here all night?" Salmon asks. "Look at you." He pats his forehead. "Like a ghost."

Tree loses the elephant creature on the horizon.

"They are the dark side of men's souls," Salmon says, motioning to the shadows. "Rowak says that all of the evil in humans exists in our shadows. It hides there, from the sunlight. After death, they used to cut the shadows off of people and lock them away deep underground. They nicknamed the underground Hell. So that the good side of every human being would go to Heaven and every bad side would go to Hell."

"What are they doing outside of Hell?" Tree asks.

"They've broken out," Salmon says. "The utopian Heaven written about in the Bible died ages ago. It's no longer a paradise. It's in ruins."

The shadows drift across the phantom landscape. Tree rubs his seashell skin patterns.

"I have a strange feeling that I'm being lied to," Tree says.

"Rowak says that the feeling is natural," Salmon says. "It took me all night getting answers out of him. He says we're like infants right now. We won't understand very much. But we'll grow."

"Did he talk about God?" Tree asks.

"He won't tell me anything about God," Salmon says. "We're probably not good enough to see Him."

Salmon rolls his finger against a seashell pattern on Tree's thigh. "He's taking us to a city after breakfast. We'll find more answers there."

Tree brushes his salmony finger away. "So how are we getting out of here?"

Salmon shrugs. The shadows fester the landscape for miles in every direction.

A large metal plate with fried chunks of lard and thick snotty sauce is smacked on the table in front of Tree. He cringes at it and pushes it away. Sitting in the enormous chair, he feels like a picky child refusing to eat his lima beans. Without any pantry in sight, Tree assumes the food has to be the pink worms from the moat.

"You'll be surprised," Salmon says, eating the slimy meat with a large fork that only half-fits into his mouth and licking the snotty sauce from his fingers.

Tree still refuses to eat.

"You could have slept in the bed with us," Rowak says. "There's room enough for five up there."

"The ladder gave me splinters," Salmon says with a full mouth.

Tree frowns at his food and takes a tiny bite of the smallest piece of meat. His face lights up, like things are popping and moving inside. The taste is overwhelming. Not necessarily good or bad, but complex and intense. Like dozens of opposing tastes are colliding at the same time. He doesn't remember there being dozens of tastes. He remembers sweet, spicy, salty, sour, bitter, what else was there? The taste of the blubbery meat is none of these yet very strong in many other ways.

"By the look on your face I can tell you've noticed the change," Rowak says.

Tree looks at him with a sagged jaw.

"Sensations are different in Heaven," Rowak says. "On Earth, they were simple and easy. Here, they are infinite. There are not only five senses anymore. There are hundreds. And each sense has billions of varieties."

"I don't notice any new senses," Tree says.

"Not yet," Rowak says. "But the five senses you had in your previous life are beginning to expand, aren't they? You are beginning to experience new flavors. You're probably seeing colors you've never seen before."

"I don't know," Tree says. "I'm not sure what is new and what I've forgotten."

"Things will be confusing for a long time," Rowak says. "You have a lot to learn."

Salmon is licking the snotty soup from his plate, his facial expression like he's licking a battery and enjoying every second of it.

Before they leave for the city, Tree has to go to the bathroom. Unfortunately, he can't find a bathroom in the fortress. Nor can he find any holes on his body to release the body waste.

"What am I supposed to do?" he asks Rowak.

Rowak goes to his bedroom and pulls a wooden bucket from the monstrous bed. The bucket has an enormous spike pointing out of it.

"Here," Rowak says. "I'll show you."

Rowak steps behind Tree and places the bucket between them. Salmon watches with giggles from the giant's chair, swinging his legs to a musical rhythm.

"What are you going to—"

Before Tree can finish, Rowak pulls him back and impales him on the wooden spike. Tree shrieks like a bat. It is not painful; it creates a sensation like sitting on a raw egg. Rowak pushes Tree upright and a syrup of white, red, and black swirls oozes out of the new hole and fills the bucket. Tree's mouth widens with shock. He feels the insides of him are different than they were before death. He is mostly goop inside. Like an insect. He is positive he was thick with internal organs during his past life.

After the syrup stops running, Rowak sews up the new hole with black thread and wipes the fluid off of his legs and crotch with an old rag. A smell like peaches mixed with dead earwigs clogs the room until Rowak dumps the bucket's contents out of the window and stows it under his bed.

"You have to do that every time," Rowak tells Tree, sitting him down on a pile of hay in the corner. "The hole will heal itself in an hour, so it must be pierced open again. Make sure to sew it every time or else it won't heal properly and you'll have waste leaking down your legs."

Tree's horrified face glares at Salmon, who doesn't seem at all bothered by watching his bathroom performance.

"You'll get used to it," Rowak says, patting Tree's shoulder.

The path is underground. Rowak opens a hatch under the giant's table and leads the two newcomers into a tiny crawl space in the earth. One by one, they trudge through muddy darkness on all fours. They aren't speaking, just heavy breaths fill the tunnel. Tree can hear the textures and shapes in his breath. He can taste the flavor of the sound it makes.

Tree searches his mind for some kind of memories. In the darkness, his thoughts are a bit more clear. He is not being swarmed with alien visions and new colors. He tries to catch things floating in his mind and hold them tight. The things he can catch are trivial, but he concentrates on them as if they're the most important of memories.

He remembers a woman laughing deeply, almost like a man, and drinking scotch. She's smoking too. He doesn't think it was anyone important in his life. Definitely not a mom or lover. Maybe a distant aunt or a neighbor. Perhaps she was just a character from a television show. He remembers television shows, but can't think of what any were called. Just faceless sitcoms with laugh tracks and kooky characters. The people talking to the woman in this memory are fuzzy and even less familiar. The memory doesn't really go any further than that. When the scotch woman speaks, her language is under water. Her cigarette smoke, spider webbed in the air, is the only smell in the room.

Tree locks onto a different memory. A memory of driving down a street in the dead of morning. The houses are all identical and comfortingly familiar. He's not sure if he is driving the car or just a passenger, but he knows he is on his way to somewhere he doesn't want to go. Kittens are crawling in and out of the windows and cuddling in his lap.

He goes to another memory. He is cutting off his fingers with a switchblade. Instead of blood, red worms are crawling out of him and squirming against the tabletop. This must be from a dream or a movie. It couldn't have really happened to him. In fact, all of these memories seem more like dreams he once had. Or perhaps they are just things his subconscious has made up for him on the spot.

It hurts him to think about the past.

The tunnel opens up into a small brick-walled room, caked with mud and ancient footprints. Piles of old clothes lie in the corners. A smell like burnt paper and chewing gum lingers in the air.

There is a lit stove cooking a pot of coffee to the left. But there isn't anybody in sight. In fact, it seems as if nobody has been here for months or years.

"Go up," Rowak tells Tree, pointing to a rusty ladder that leads to a hatch in the ceiling.

Tree stares up the rusted ladder. "What about those things?"

Rowak pushes at him. "It is safe up there. A river keeps the shadows back."

Tree climbs a few rungs and then pauses.

Salmon is pouring the pot of coffee into metal cups. He finds some grayish sugar in an old boot under the stove.

"Move it," Rowak says, and Tree continues up the ladder.

They emerge into a field of white turtle-shaped flowers growing in zigzagged patterns. A wide but shallow river is behind them, pink-colored due to worm content.

"You still have your shadow," Tree tells Rowak. "It wasn't cut off?"

23

"It's been a long time since a shadow has been removed," Rowak says. "The technology has long been forgotten."

"Tell him about the multiple shadows," Salmon says.

Rowak nods at Salmon with steel teeth and tells Tree, "It is important to never let one of the stray shadows latch onto you. They will attach themselves to your soul and become a part of you. Then you will have two dark sides. Yours and somebody else's."

"And there's no limit to how many shadows can attach themselves to you," Salmon interjects.

"There are some locked deep underground who are connected to twenties of shadows. Their souls pumped with the evils of so many men that they have become mad with hate and despair. None of the new ones know how to remove shadows, so we must lock away these lost souls and forget them."

"Is anyone without a shadow?" Tree asks.

"Not any of the new ones," Rowak says. "The old ones had the technology to remove shadows. There aren't any old ones left."

"Old ones?" Tree asks.

"The old ones are those who lived before the fall of Heaven. We call ourselves the new ones."

"There has to be somebody who knows about the old ones," Tree says.

"The old ones disappeared long before the new ones came," Rowak says.

"What about God?" Tree says. "Did He disappear as well?"

"Of course God did not disappear," Rowak says. "He is God."

"Then why don't you ask Him to teach you the ways of the old ones?" Tree asks.

Rowak just laughs and wobbles an elbow. "Children…"

CHAPTER THREE

The city is like a pile of dirty old boots in the distance. It looks old and dead, as quiet and motionless as a painting. Even the small strings of smoke from crooked chimneys appear to be at a standstill.

In another direction, there are golden crab-like creatures as tall as houses creeping through the trees. To get a better view Salmon climbs a hill of wagon wheels that have become part of the soil, spilling drops of hot coffee on his thighs. The sight of the creatures gives Tree sour beeskin sensations down his back.

"What are they?" Salmon asks.

Rowak pokes at the ground with a curly stick.

"What do you think they are?"

"Crab dinosaurs," Salmon says, rubbing a thigh.

"There are three of them," Rowak says. "There have always been three of them."

Tree takes a few steps up the pile of wagon wheels.

"Can we get a closer look?"

"No," Rowak says. "Anyone who gets too close will be killed."

Salmon spills more of his coffee on himself.

"Killed?" Salmon says. "You mean we can still be killed?"

"I thought we were immortal," Tree says.

Rowak pokes at balloon-flowers until they pop.

"Nothing is immortal," Rowak says.

"But we're in Heaven," Salmon says. "The Bible says we'll live forever in Heaven."

"The Bible was written by people who had never been to Heaven," Rowak says. "After you died on Earth, your soul did not become immortal. It just changed." He sits down in the mud. Razorblade butterflies flutter around his left ear. "It escaped your old body through a doorway in the back of your brain and arrived here, where it was made flesh. You do not age in Heaven. But eventually you will die."

"What happens after we die in Heaven?" Salmon asks. "Does our soul leave this body and go to another place?"

"No," Rowak says. "The body you are in is your soul made flesh. Once this flesh dies, your soul will end."

"I'll just die?" Salmon asks. "Forever?"

"You'll just end," Rowak says.

Salmon hides behind pickled bushes to make sure the crab creatures don't see him.

The town still looks kind of like a pile of old boots on arrival. The houses are made of stone and clay, lopsided, melting into the earth. There is an iron gate wrapped around the buildings covered in green rust and a dark blob of cloud directly overhead like a warm canopy.

Tree rubs his square nostrils as a sweetly rotten gooseberry smell hits the air. "It looks deserted," he says, even though there are dim lights in several of the buildings beyond the gate.

"New ones," Rowak calls out to a cone tower above.

The tower is black. Every brick in the tower seems to be a centimeter away from falling out, all at once. It doesn't look like anyone could possibly stand up there without collapsing the structure.

"How long has it been since you were here last?" Tree asks.

Rowak waits a few minutes before he responds, staring up at the window with an O mouth.

"There are only a handful of people living on the surface," he says. "It always looks dead."

A long wait, with Salmon clacking his empty coffee cups together and wobbling his hips to the rhythm, and Tree lying in green mud with his hand over his eyes.

"She's waking up," Rowak says to a very dim light in the blackness of the tower.

An azure woman appears at the window. Her body wrapped in a blanket.

"A couple newcomers," Rowak tells her. "Can you believe it? Two at once!"

The azure woman: tiny black holes for eyes, glaring like a gargoyle down at them…

"It's been a long time since any new arrivals have come," Rowak tells her. "I've been getting lonely out there all by myself. Can you believe there's two of them?"

Rowak pauses for an answer but the woman does not speak. Her lurid stare twitches a nerve down Tree's spine like an eel under his skin. Rowak is shaking. He's nervous for some reason. He doesn't look at the azure woman in the face.

"I wonder why nobody ever comes anymore," Rowak continues. "It's been so long. I don't think people are able to find the doorway in the backs of their heads anymore."

Another pause. He waits for her to speak.

It takes several moments, Tree rubbing green mud on his fingernails, then:

"How many times do I have to tell you?" her voice crackles and bubbles.

Rowak shivers.

"Don't bring me any pinkies," she says.

Rowak looks at Salmon. "He's not pink. He's much more red than pink. He's salmon-colored."

"He's pink enough," the woman says.

"What's wrong with pink?" Salmon asks, stretching his neck out at them like a snail.

"Nobody likes people with pink skin," Rowak tells him.

"What?" Salmon cries. "You're judging me by the color of my skin?"

"There's racism in Heaven?" Tree asks.

"Everyone is judged by the color of their skin here," Rowak says. "Your skin color is the color of your soul. Some types of souls are less popular than others. Pink souls are by far the least popular of them all."

"Pink represents annoying and irritating," the woman creaks.

"You are only about half pink," Rowak tells Salmon. "I didn't think they would make you go underground for being only half pink."

Salmon cries, "What do you mean go underground?"

Rowak avoids Salmon's gaze, frowning. He looks up at the tower window but the woman is no longer there.

"Anyone they want to forget about they put underground," Rowak says.

"But I'm not annoying!" Salmon says.

"I don't know you enough to judge," Rowak says. "But your soul is pinkish and all pink souls belong to annoying people."

Salmon rubs at his skin as if trying to rub the pink off.

Tree says, "But what is annoying to one person might be endearing to others. It's like saying blue skin represents beauty or red skin represents good fashion sense. It's all a matter of opinion."

"It's not just a matter of opinion," Rowak says.

The woman arrives in the nude. Just like the others, she doesn't have any privates. She has breasts but there aren't any nipples attached to them. She is taller than all the men, almost twice their height. And she has two sets of arms. The back of her head is like that of a triceratops. And the markings on her skin are chaotic, like a violent abstract painting. Not a symmetric pattern like the men's flesh.

She opens the gate and locks her pinhole eyes on Tree.

"A yellow?" she asks.

"Yes," Rowak hyper-nods. "Isn't it wonderful?"

"What does yellow represent?" Tree asks.

The woman's neck moves machine-like to Rowak. "Why don't you ever tell them anything?"

Rowak crouches. "Mystery is more fun."

"All the questions you fail to answer just come to me," she

says. "Making my job so much more difficult."

The azure lady bends down to Tree and whispers against his cheek with thin oily lips. "Yellow is special."

The interior of the town is like walking into a smooth ceramic dish with powder mites and mulch barrels polluting the otherwise spotless surface. Powder mites are wobbling rat-sized fleas that make fizzy noises and excrete piles of grayish dust along the waffle-iron sidewalks. The azure lady doesn't mind crushing them with her dinosaur feet, coating her blue heels with orange mucus.

Beady-eyes peek out of melty windows, glaring at them. The citizens have frozen facial expressions. They are like large porcelain dolls. Some of them wear wigs and cartoon makeup, to look more human, to cover up the true appearance of their souls.

"What is wrong with them?" Salmon whispers to Tree.

Tree tries not to look at the scary doll people glaring down at them. Their mechanical faces tilting only slightly to follow their movements. Footsteps sound like peppery saliva in Tree's new ears.

"Get rid of the pink one," Azure Woman says to Rowak. "I'll take the yellow."

Rowak nods and leads the pinkish man in another direction. Tree and Salmon stare at each other with broken eyes and clogged throats. Lizard tongues darting in and out of Salmon's nostrils.

"You don't need him," the woman whispers to Tree. "You're a yellow."

The majority of the town looks destroyed, as if burned down centuries ago. The dead buildings are like rotten fruit scattered across the landscape. Only a small section of town is still occupied. Only a couple dozen souls live here.

They leave the small circle of old boot buildings and enter the black ruins, thick with ash and crispy whispers. There is a small trail cutting through the charred sculptures, tiny flappy mice leading the way.

"Are all towns in Heaven this quiet?" Tree asks.

"There aren't many towns in Heaven," the azure lady says. "The capital city is the largest. It is where God lives. But nobody goes there anymore. It is forbidden."

"Have you ever met God?" Tree asks.

She glares at him with her hole-eyes.

"Do you have any memory of your old world?" she asks.

"Not really," Tree says.

"Good. It's better that you forget about the old world and concentrate on the new. Some of your past will come back to you eventually, but for now it'll just get in the way."

Tree nods.

The trail ends at a black wall. Not so much a wall as a bunch of scraps of burnt wood nailed together into a sheet.

"Come," she says, opening the wood scraps like a door, "I will buy you a drink."

The tall blue woman ducks down into the dark structure, hot liquids twisting under her skin as she bends to fit inside, pulling on Tree with her extra set of arms.

Inside it is damp and dim, a patchwork of charcoal wood and chunks of rust-sticky metal. A pub. Debris scraps woven violently together to form a new structure out of the black ruins. A lounge, containing three or four people with drinks, making little noise, just the sound of arms rustling and sweat leaking down ashy pig backs.

Hundreds of nails of all sizes point down from the ceiling like metal icicles. The chairs and tables: a roller coaster of rotten wood and thick spikes. The furniture is not gigantic as it was in Rowak's home. It will fit Tree perfectly, but is a little small for the azure woman.

She says her name is CLOTTA, pronounced in all capital letters. Tree asks if CLOTTA is short for anything and

CLOTTA says she needs a drink.

CLOTTA sits Tree down at the bar in a lumpy blond chair made of finger-thick splinters. They cut into his yellow flesh and make him feel like an autumn oak leaf wrapped around a chocolate-filled wasp. CLOTTA needs two to support her enormous mass.

The other people in the bar are all swollen eyeballs at Tree. Looking at him with chubbed cheeks and leaky face paint. They appear to be aroused and disgusted by Tree at the same time, flapping their ears and elbow-tails at him.

"Two donkabies," CLOTTA says to the fish-silver bartender, who grunts with a melty warthog chin and rolling belly fat.

Then CLOTTA places a finger on the bartender's wrist. A few grams of flesh rise up from the azure woman's palm and crawl up her hand, onto the Bartender's arm. It changes into a silver color and sinks into his flesh, becomes a part of him.

"What was that?" Tree asks CLOTTA as the bartender pours greasy fluid into bone-white cups.

"I gave him a piece of my soul," she responds. "Soul is the only thing of value we have in Heaven, so we use it as our currency."

"You trade with flesh?" Tree asks.

"Soul-flesh," she says. "You give people some of your soul-flesh for their products or services and then you take soul-flesh for products and services you provide."

"What if someone doesn't have any products or services?" Tree asks.

"Then they become very small," CLOTTA says. "There is always something you can do, but every once in a while there are the lazy ones. These people will eventually lose all of their soul-flesh and be completely consumed. Usually by Jeke here," the bartender nods his portly neck, "or myself. We are the largest people in town. The wealthiest."

"What services do you provide?" Tree asks.

"I am the caretaker," CLOTTA says. "Everyone pays me taxes to live in my town. If you don't have extra soul-flesh at the end of every month I will completely absorb you into me. Your soul will become my soul and you will no longer exist."

She takes a gulp of the greasy beverage.

"Drink," she says, pointing to the lumpy mug. "It'll be the only free drink you ever get."

Tree scoops out the thick sleep-textured goo with two fingers and presses it to his tongue. It tastes like cherry pine mixed with Detroit cops arresting a pregnant prostitute. Like other flavors in Heaven, it is more disturbing and confusing than it is disgusting. After a few sips, Tree begins to feel the effects. It is not the same as alcohol. It makes the insides of his flesh whirl into tiny circles. Like he's getting thousands of miniature massages from the inside out. It has a calming effect on his entire soul. He understands why people would spend a lot of their soul-flesh here, even if the taste/texture of the fluid is unfriendly.

CLOTTA allows Tree to enjoy his new sensations for some moments. She watches as his eyes focus into the deep pores of the counter top, at the magnificent textures. He carefully examines his yellow skin and finds new details in his soul-flesh: there are cityscape patterns within the seashell patterns, and dragon scale patterns within the cityscape patterns, with multiple colors hiding behind the yellow, multiple textures that his senses can hardly process.

His new body is a complex web of art.

Tree is so captivated by his skin that he doesn't even notice an obese winged infant flop-flying into the pub and sitting down next to him. It orders a small drink and masturbates.

The azure woman purchases a tube of tightly packed yarn and places it delicately next to her drink when something shiny catches her eye. It is attached to Tree's elbow.

"What is this?" she says, leaning down to Tree and grabbing his arm with all four of her hands.

Tree oozes into her grip and smiles.

She pulls on the shiny metal tag sticking out of his elbow and out comes a handleless blade as long as Tree's forearm.

"This is unusual," CLOTTA says, examining the intricately designed blade. It is more stylized than his flesh, with battle-scenes carved into the metal. "I have never heard of someone sneaking a weapon into Heaven before."

"Why was it inside me?" Tree asks.

"Perhaps it's just part of your soul," CLOTTA says, sliding the blade back into Tree's arm. "People have been born with wheels attached to their feet, with televisions in their bellies. I've even heard of a little girl who was born into Heaven with toys buried deep in her torso. But I never thought a weapon would come through."

"It's just a knife," Tree says.

"It's a symbol of power," CLOTTA says, wrapping her arms around his neck. "You're going to make an excellent addition to our community."

Tree doesn't respond. He shrinks in his seat as she stares down at him with a spider-smile on her big blue face.

"So what does yellow mean?"

"Imagination," she says. "Yellow is the color of art, music, poetry. Yellow is the color of creation. We have been waiting a very long time for a yellow to join our community."

"I don't remember being a creative person."

"That doesn't matter. You will be our new entertainer. I'm sure you'll come up with all sorts of creative ways to make us happy. Even if you didn't live a life as an artist, it is in your soul. We will all benefit from your imagination."

Tree notices the masturbating baby seated next to him. It looks up at him with a toothless grin and gurgles.

"It's an angel," CLOTTA says over Tree's shoulder.

"What's an angel?" Tree says. He doesn't remember that part of the Bible.

"Angels were God's first inventions, created long before humans. Heavily flawed. Not good enough to be the children of Earth, so He tossed them aside and forgot about them. They don't have language or very much intelligence. Their limbs hardly work. They are not very good for anything."

"Why is it masturbating?" Tree asks.

"It isn't masturbating. It doesn't have any sex organs. The penis-shaped tube it is jerking on is actually an air pump. It has to constantly pump air into its lungs in order to breathe."

"How many of them are there?"

"Not many. Most have died off. Those that remain are preserved and protected. They are our only connection to Heaven's past and we hope one day we'll learn how to communicate with them."

Tree watches the obese baby/angel masturbate its air pump and guzzle its beverage.

"You don't know Heaven's past?" Tree asks.

"Much is still a mystery to us," CLOTTA says. "It was a belief on Earth that after you die all of the questions you ever had would get answered. But, in actuality, after death very few answers are given and a whole lot more questions are asked. You will have to learn to live without all the answers."

"I have many questions," Tree says.

"Save them for later," CLOTTA says. "I will get you a mentor in the morning. He will be able to answer more questions than I am willing."

CLOTTA finishes both of their drinks and grabs the tube of yarn with her lower right hand.

"Join me out back," she says.

The goblin baby drools at them with steel ball eyes.

Outside with spiky curls of wind, CLOTTA lights her tube of yarn like a cigar with a pinching of her fingertips. She is made of lightning. The cigar isn't really made of yarn but ropes of tobacco woven together. Each rope of tobacco is a different color and flavor. The flavors are too complex for Tree to taste correctly, so she does not waste her smoke on the newcomer.

Tree doesn't mind the smoking giant. He is busy examining the black graveyard of city ahead. Rows of charred blob-buildings slide down the throat of a silver forest less than a mile away. Beyond the forest is a small gated village on top of a mushroom hill. There are lights emanating from the village. Just a faint sign of life.

"What is that place over there?" Tree asks.

"There is nothing there," CLOTTA says.

"I see a village on that hill in the distance," Tree says.

"There's no village. The only other populated city in Heaven is miles away in the other direction."

"I see it right there."

"You are mistaken."

Tree squints at the village in the distance. It is clearly there. Lights are on in the buildings. There is a silent twitch in CLOTTA's face.

"I don't think I'll be very entertaining," Tree says to CLOTTA.

"You will be. You're yellow."

"But I don't feel like a yellow."

"It doesn't really matter, does it?"

"I don't know what to do."

"It'll come to you. I have faith."

"What if I'm not entertaining?"

"Then you will be poor."

"Can't I get another job?"

"No, this is your job."

Tree sneers.

"If you don't do the job you won't be able to pay rent and I'll be forced to absorb you."

CHAPTER FOUR

CLOTTA takes Tree to a party. She doesn't bother asking him if he wants to go. Two of her enormous arms wrap around his neck and pull him through town like a child on a leash.

"These are the people you will want to get to know," she tells him. "They are the upper class."

She leads him into one of the old blackened buildings, up spongy-wood stairs that his feet sink into with each step.

It smells like blind cats in here. The lighting is dark brown. The flowery wallpaper is black and scratchy.

"Only speak when spoken to," CLOTTA whispers.

Inside of a small room at the top of the stairs, there are five portly women and a man sitting in a circle. Like many of the other townspeople, they are dressed up like old porcelain dolls. Covered in thick layers of makeup. Fluffy pink and yellow dresses.

All of them sit there, on the floor or on top of old decaying mattresses, just staring at each other. Their faces painted into a permanent smile between plump rosy cheeks.

Tree wonders if they actually are adult-sized dolls until he sees their eyes moving within the makeup.

CLOTTA sits Tree down next to the male. He is twice the size of Tree, dressed as a fat German boy with a curly mustache painted onto his lip.

The man twists his head mechanically until it faces Tree. He stares at him for several minutes with bloodshot eyes. Then twists back to face the ladies. There are cracks in his makeup. Tree can see his greasy gray skin beneath, pulsating and emitting a strong coppery odor.

CLOTTA doesn't sit. She stands in the doorway, crouched over with her arms spread out like a spider.

Nobody speaks.

For hours, Tree sits there with them, watching them stare at each other. They occasionally move their heads, cracking their make-up, to stare at Tree. But the yellow man ignores them.

The situation is cutting deep into his nerves. Tree pretends he is not in the room with them. He lowers his head and closes his eyes, but he can still feel their eyeballs pressed against his skin whenever they turn to stare.

Tree wakes to CLOTTA pushing on his back with her heavy raptor foot. He opens his eyes. All of the doll people are gone. He is lying on one of the old crusty mattresses. Cobwebs cover his face like he has been asleep here for decades. For some reason, he's still tired.

"It's time to go," CLOTTA says. "You can't stay here."

She pulls him out of the bed and leads his staggering body downstairs into the street.

Rowak is in the center of the town with stacks of popping fuzz-balls in his arms. He is collecting them from a vinegar barrel and sucking the vinegar-like fluid out of the fur. The fuzz-balls pop and flip at him like puppies.

"Did you drop him?" CLOTTA asks Rowak.

Rowak backs away and cowers, as if he's doing something wrong with the fuzz-balls. "Yes, yes. He has joined the lower depths. How is the yellow working out?"

"We'll see," says the azure woman.

"Where will he stay? With the Carrols?"

"Not this time," she says. "He'll stay at the Topo House."

Rowak goes limp and the fuzz-balls roll out of his hands.

"The… Topo House?" he says. "You can't let him stay there. He's too new."

"I want him to understand our ways. That won't happen if he's sheltered like a baby."

"But the Topo House…"

"And I want you to take him there."

"But I…"

"Take him to the most suitable room and then go back to your dolls."

CLOTTA bows her massive torso at them and walks away. Long blue arms liquid-swaying as she returns to the gatehouse.

Rowak straightens his back and smooths the tightness in his face. He becomes the pseudo-wiseman that he was outside of town. Tree, wondering which character is the real Rowak, asks him if CLOTTA makes him nervous. Rowak just answers the question with a question, another useless rhetorical question that makes him feel superior.

The Topo House doesn't look very different from the other rotten houses in the village—Rowak approaches slowly, again losing his grip on the wiseman persona—but it feels different.

Tree is beginning to experience another sense coming through. Not sight or smell. It is very slight, but what Tree is sensing from the Topo House is something like boiling baby fat mixed with a wig of razor-hair slicing up the back of his neck. It is the sixth sense. Not a psychic sense, as the sixth sense was defined on Earth. Something much more tangible. Like sound. But Tree is having difficulty processing it.

"Good luck," Rowak tells Tree, locking his legs.

"Aren't you taking me in?" Tree asks.

Rowak shakes his head. "There will be a room to the right of the nail paintings. Just go in the room. Get into bed and go to sleep. Ignore anything you see."

They stare at each other for a moment.

"Don't move until somebody comes to get you in the morning," Rowak says.

Pecan vomit emotions as Tree enters the Topo House. Rowak slams the door between them with click-scurries and a whimper. The room is dark gray chaos. A war zone. It overwhelms Tree, too much for his virgin mind to process. He sees spiked vibrating balls and greasy swollen penis-tubes clogging the open space. Spicy lard sounds in the air.

Tree takes the only open path through the warm meat-machinery, looking down at his feet. He needs to find the nail paintings but does not know what nail paintings are or how he'll be able to tell them apart from this mess.

Getting dizzy and covered in a film of plastic fluid, Tree pushes forward. His path is lit by several metal buckets containing small blobs of breathing warm meat. The meat glows and jitters at Tree as he passes. No nail paintings anywhere or even anything remotely resembling a painting, so Tree takes the first right-hand door he can find. The doors here open like dresser drawers. Tree has to climb in and pull it shut. His new flesh rubbery against the aluminum.

Inside: it is more like a closet than a room. With piles of ropes and mops and strange webby devices. Lit by only a few random blobs of meat.

Half the room is occupied by a giant bed. Or at least Tree thinks it is a bed. It is shaped like a bed but instead of a mattress there is a tub filled with an odd substance that can only be described as a cross between heart burn and dying elephant cries.

"Sick," Tree mumbles.

He examines the pile of junk and digs out a plastic tarp and some netting. He lays it in the small open space of floor between the tub/bed and the cluttered junk. And attempts to do as Rowak suggested—go right to sleep.

But first: he stands in the middle of the room frozen like a statue for a few hours…

His flesh becomes powdery as he gets into the netting/tarp bed and the hard metal floor makes him feel like sandy feathers. But eventually he falls asleep.

Drifting in and out of sleep...

He's not really sure how to sleep anymore. He has no idea what being comfortable or uncomfortable is supposed to feel like. There are noises all around him. Gurgles and pepper-poppings. Sometimes he can taste ripped up pieces of paper in the air.

A deep sleep.

Then wide awake again as a spiral creature opens the drawer to his room and stretch-dances up the walls around him.

Tree can feel it examining his body. He feels like his soul is being flipped through like a filing cabinet. The drawer/door closes but Tree no longer feels alone/safe here.

He keeps his eyes closed and blanks his mind out as hard as he can until he is again asleep.

A twitching in his nostrils chokes Tree awake, looking around the room like somebody did something to him. He sneezes into his palm. A chunk of black and gray. Tree pokes at it and it moves. It grows legs and crawls up his finger. A squid spider. Tree flicks it away.

A pain attacks Tree's belly. A pain that he actually recognizes. Gas pains. He has to go to the bathroom.

"Not now," he says, holding his belly and scanning the area for one of those toilet contraptions that Rowak introduced him to. Nothing like it in the junk pile.

"There must be something I can use."

He digs through the odd tools and scraps until he finds a tin can similar to a coffee can. No, exactly like a coffee can. He empties it of glitter dust and sets it on the floor. Without realizing what he's doing, he whips the ornate blade out of his arm and cuts open his crotch.

Tree squats and a ball of gook splats into the coffee can, not too worried about missing the sides. It oozes out of him and the gas pains slowly disappear.

Just as he sighs in relief, he feels the ooze of waste dripping up his thighs and sliding up his back. It wraps around his sides and warms his belly.

Tree looks down and grabs a handful of the waste from his belly. Squid spiders. Dozens of them, squirming in his hand. He realizes that it's all squid spiders coming out of him. The coffee can is filled with them, the ground is swarming with them. They are crawling all over him.

He freezes. Eyes tearing. A tornado of snot in the back of his throat.

He calmly decides to go insane.

Racing out of the Topo House screaming at the top of his crackling white wine lungs, thrashing at the puddles of squid spiders on the back of his thighs. They are still coming out of him.

He just runs. Aimlessly out of the village and into the blue-black night. He doesn't want to be in Heaven anymore. He doesn't want to live in the Topo House or try to entertain the people of CLOTTA's town.

Tree circles behind silent buildings and squeezes between brick walls until he finds himself in the old dead section of the city, behind the scrapheap tavern, facing the small village on the hill in the distance.

That's where Tree wants to be. It looks more civilized and friendly. The lights of the town brighten the landscape like a beacon. And CLOTTA acting like it doesn't exist only makes Tree want to see it even more.

It's got to be a better town than this one, he thinks.

He wipes at the spiders on his back one last time and then follows the thin trail through the ruins.

There is a memory of a man touching Tree's penis. It flashes in and out of his head without his permission. Tree is a child or maybe a teenager, he can't tell. But he knows the man is very large. His hands like hairy bricks. Again, Tree isn't really sure if this ever happened to him during his life, but he can feel it clearly. He is suffocated by the man's musky flavor. His mass of sweaty heat and gray chest hair. His face is blurred but Tree can remember a bald head with freckles and peeling flakes of scalp. Tree doesn't know why he's with the man but he knows he doesn't want to be there anymore. The memory makes Tree sick. It is something he shouldn't be remembering. Something he doesn't want to remember. He hopes it was just a bad dream he had a long time ago.

The town is much farther than Tree realized. He has been walking for hours now and doesn't feel any closer than when he began.

His legs are feeling like twisted ladders and his eyes droop sore. There are still squid spiders dripping out of the gash in his crotch.

The black graveyard of city ends and Tree enters a cool plain of lime-green. The ground is oddly flat and smooth here, like he's walking on a glass tabletop. There is no longer any vegetation around him. It still looks like ground but it is flat. Two-dimensional. Tree continues towards the hill on the flatland. It's too late to turn back. He's got to get to the new city. But after a few dozen feet, Tree realizes that the horizon is also flat. He comes to the end of the landscape and realizes he's at a wall. The distance is painted on. It's not real. The village on the hill doesn't really exist. It's just part of an enormous painting that reaches to the top of the sky.

Tree presses against the picture and it expands to the length of his arm. It's flexible. Like canvas paper but rubbery like a balloon. He releases his hand and the landscape bounces back at him. The lights from the village are really flickering. There is movement in the bushes on the hills, movement of carriages in the town, but it's all part of a picture. It's all some kind of illusion, some kind of movie to trick people from far away. Tree looks back to CLOTTA's town. It is very far. He just now realizes how far he's gone. Has he gone to the edge of Heaven? He is in a corner. Perhaps Heaven is within a giant box. The inner walls of the box just moving pictures.

Tree realizes his blade has been in his hand this whole time. He is beginning to feel an unusual connection between him and the knife. He wonders if CLOTTA is right. He thinks maybe it is an extension of his body, his soul. Though it also seems to have a life of its own as it stabs into the landscape screen and cuts a slit all the way down to the floor. Tree widens the hole and slips his head through, like peeking out from under the covers.

What Tree sees he does not at all understand. Whatever it is, it is vast. His brain processes it as an ocean of computer networks but he knows that it is something far more complex than that. There are waterfalls of electrical fluids. Millions of miles of circuits and wires. It stretches farther than his eyes can see in every direction. Perhaps it is the machinery that powers Heaven. Perhaps the world he is within isn't Heaven at all.

It takes Tree the rest of the night and some of the morning to walk back to town. As he arrives, CLOTTA and many of the townspeople are standing in a mob waiting for him. Like they knew what he had done. CLOTTA stands like a blue demon among a mob of doll-faced people.

"You are not to wander," CLOTTA says.

Tree is unable to speak.

"We will have to start locking you up at--"

CLOTTA freezes, her pinhole eyes examining Tree's feet. She approaches him. Shakes her head at him.

"You stupid man," she says, staring at his feet and shaking her head. "You stupid, stupid man."

"What?" Tree says.

She points at his feet. "You've picked up an extra shadow."

Tree looks down. There is only his normal shadow.

"No, I didn't. This is the shadow I've always had."

"There is a small one hiding within your shadow," she says.

Tree looks down again and for a moment sees a shadow of a little girl with pigtails peeking out from behind his shadow.

"Look what you've done," CLOTTA says. "You've ruined everything. Why couldn't you stay put and do what you're told?"

"I couldn't stay in that place another second," Tree says. "You never should have made me stay there."

"Don't speak to me," CLOTTA says. "You're dead to this town. We're sending you underground."

"But I don't feel any different," Tree says. "I don't feel more evil than I did."

"If you have more than one shadow you must go underground. Those are the rules."

"But I haven't changed."

"Those are the rules."

Rowak escorts Tree away from the mob. There is a look of compassion on his face, but Tree isn't sure if the look is forged or genuine.

"You really upset her," Rowak says. "It was a horrible thing you did."

"I was scared," Tree says.

"There was nothing to be scared of. There are no dangers within town. You just didn't understand your environment. But now you have reason to be afraid. The underground is a cruel and ugly place. As soon as you go down there it will be a constant fight for survival. You'll be lucky to last longer than five minutes."

44

Rowak leads Tree to a gated courtyard. Vines with 5-inch razor thorns grow up the walls and gates, organic razorwire. In the center of the courtyard is a manhole. Rowak untwists the heavy iron lid and opens it. A rising of warm vapors from within and a smell like orange pavement. Tree peers down into the dark. He can't see the bottom. There is no ladder or rope leading down.

"How am I supposed to get down there?" Tree asks.

"How do you think you're supposed to get down there?" Rowak says, sadly.

"It won't hurt will it?" Tree asks.

Rowak looks down and pretends to measure the distance to the bottom, but doesn't give a reply. He pats Tree's shoulder a good luck and half-smiles at him, then pushes him over the edge. Ass first down the hole.

CHAPTER FIVE

Tree wakes in soft warm black. Crab-moisture in the air burns his lungs. His vision clears and he's able to see in the dark. Cat-eyes glowing.

He's in an enormous cavern. The ceiling is like the inside of a whale. The floor like wet meaty tongue-tissue. The walls are too far away for him to see.

His yellow flesh is covered in tiny multi-colored mounds. Ticks. Digging into his skin and sucking his fluids. They grow plumper by the second. More of them are crawling out of the tongue-flesh carpet and crawling onto his limbs and waist. He brushes at them but they are in deep. He has to pick them out one by one.

The last of them crawls out of his fingers and attempts to reenter his skin on the back of his hand. It wiggles a plump blue butt at him. Tree's eyes widen at the little creature. It's not a tick. None of them are ticks. They are tiny people, hungry for soul-flesh.

The little blue one is female, with four breasts and porcupine hair. She catches Tree's glare and freezes, stares back with hollow wooden eyes. Her face becomes soggy, drooping at him. A wooden moan screeches out of her black tar mouth.

Before Tree gets a chance to flick her away, his flesh absorbs her. Yellow veins climb her limbs and pull her down into his knuckles. Her face becomes a yellow molten blob gurgling bubbles out of stretchy lips as he involuntarily takes her inside of him. He tries to pull her out but she is already just blue and green paint swirling deep into the back of his hand.

Deep rumbling growls steal his attention.

He whips the blade out of his skin and poses, ready to attack, as he examines the area. He is expecting dozens of multi-shadowed evil men to jump out at him and try to rob him of his soul-flesh.

Examining his surroundings:

The entire cave is made of meat. Moist bladder walls, bubbled mounds of tongue. A texture like rotten death flesh.

The cave stretches for miles. Empty of life except for the dozens of tiny tick-people that hop at his feet. He walks in the direction that looks the flattest, careful not to slip. His blade raised above his head.

For hours, he travels the meaty underworld, searching for other people. But there is only a thick black hairy smell here.

"Salmon," Tree calls out.

No response. He's not surprised.

Soon he comes to a skeleton's arm on the ground. People don't have bones in Heaven so he's not quite sure where it could have come from. Actually, it couldn't be human. It is much too long and the fingers end in razor sharp claws. He's pretty sure humans did not have razor sharp claws.

Tree continues through the slippery meat until he finds another skeleton arm. Then another. There is a trail of them that leads him to a whole field of the skeleton arms.

And beyond that: a lake of sweat.

There is something moving near the shore. Tree steps closer, his blade itching in his palm. It is some kind of creature. A blob of flesh, a large womb creature with three skeletal arms growing out of its guts.

The creature picks tiny people/ticks off of the bank of the sweat pool and drops them into its goo-hole mouth. Tree can hear micro shrieks from a pink tick-woman flapping her limbs as she is sucked into black blubbery lips and swallowed.

The pudding blob groans and gurgles at the tiny people. There seems to be an unending supply of them. Tree attempts to sneak by while it eats but his movement catches the beast's black ball eyes. It drops the little people and rips across the tonguescape on centipede legs, screeching at Tree with outstretched skeletal arms.

Tree points his blade at it and the creature pauses.

"Stay back," he says.

The thing looks like it might have once been human. It might even understand him. The creature circles around Tree, traps him against the water bank. Belch-shrilling at him.

In a blink, the creature's arm is cut off as it slashes at Tree.

Tree doesn't realize that he just defended himself with the blade. It is like his subconscious controls the knife, as the creature attacks again and the knife slices off the other two skeletal limbs lightning-fast. He can cut through bones like wax.

The yellow man smiles at the armless creature, dances at it.

"I'm not so easy, am I?" Tree says, giggling at himself, in complete jubilance over his newly discovered abilities.

The creature unfolds four more arms from its blob-body and lunges forward.

Tree cuts through the bones, knocking them off at the elbow. But for every arm he cuts, another regrows. Tree's slashing movement becomes too fast to see, a whirlwind that makes a crystal hum. Limbs pile up around them. Tree has to shield his eyes from the chips of bone.

The blob slices at Tree's arm in a funny angle and almost hits his blade out of his hand. Since that arm is controlled by his subconscious, it was able to jerk away just in time. But while dodging, another arm cuts into Tree's chest. Another stabs into his belly. A long sickle arm swings out of the creature's back and cuts through Tree's ankle like a stalk of corn.

He tumbles back and splashes into the water. His severed foot lying on the shore.

The yellow man flaps his millipede tongue at the wetness and rises to one knee. The water isn't deep. He can see into his open leg. It is mostly hollow. Sodium foams out of the hole like blood.

The creature doesn't enter the liquid. It stretches out its arms and gurgle-roars.

Tree stares into the creature's black ball eyes and inches slowly forward. The creature inches slowly back. Once his big toe reaches the bank, Tree springs at the blob's face and slashes at its eyes. The blade misses by a hair. And as Tree flings himself backward the demon catches him with a single claw-finger in the pit of Tree's throat.

He slides back into the pool. Sitting on his butt and fingering the gash on his neck. It would have been deep enough to open his jugular if he still had one.

Tree backs away. He goes deeper into the sweat lake, away from the meaty snowman. The creature lowers its arms and watches carefully, but does not pursue him.

Why doesn't it follow? Tree wonders.

He smells the liquid. He wonders if it is poison. It stings his open wounds. Definitely not safe to drink but perhaps safe enough to wade through for now. Hopefully there isn't anything more deadly lurking within the water.

Tree crawls through the spicy fluid, swims through when it is deep enough, trying to find dry land.

He hears whispering but he's unsure which direction it comes from. It could just be echoes of his splashing steps. But the closer he gets to the end of the cave, the louder the whispers become.

The whispers turn to voices.

Human voices.

Tree sees them. At the end of the cave, against the meaty wall, there are two figures. One is on a tiny mound rising out of the water. The other is lying in the water at the foot of the mound.

The two figures stop speaking and watch Tree as he splashes near.

"Tree?" Salmon says, as Tree arrives. "It is him."

Salmon is the figure in the water. He says, "Hey, Tree. Look. I'm shrinking."

Salmon has a big smile as he stands up to show Tree his new size. He is now twice as thin and the height of a ten year old boy. But other than that, he's the same Salmon.

The other figure pops up and raises its skeletal arm.

Tree whips the knife out of his skin and balances on one knee.

"Stay back," the figure says.

It is a woman. A teenage-sized girl holding one of the blob-creature's detached limbs as a weapon. She is a cool green color with seahorse-textured skin and spidery vortex patterns.

"She won't share," Salmon says to Tree in a tittering pout, pointing at the tiny dry island the girl stands on.

"Where are we?" Tree says, holding his neck, his voice crackling and full of sodium.

The girl swings at his words like they are invaders.

"Welcome to Heaven's stomach," Salmon says. "All the unwanted ones are thrown down here to be digested. Recycled into fuel for Heaven's machines."

"Rowak didn't tell me anything about this," Tree gurgles.

"Rowak doesn't know anything," the girl says. "Rowak is a child just like you."

"He likes to pretend he's all grown up," Salmon says. "He has a crush on the blue woman up there and wants to appear wise and mature for her."

"CLOTTA doesn't know much more than Rowak," the green girl says. "She has never left the town since her arrival in Heaven. The people up there are too afraid to venture outside of the city gates. They all live in ignorance."

The green girl curls her eyebrows at Tree like everything is his fault.

"Her name is Swan," Salmon says. "Isn't she cute?"

The girl kicks at Salmon.

"Swan?" Tree says. "You look more like a spiky fish than a swan."

"A cute spiky fish," Salmon says, swimming in the digestive fluid.

Tree tries to stand up but he can't balance on only one foot.

"What happened to you?" Salmon asks his ankle.

"That thing," Tree says, looking back.

"It's some kind of guardian of the stomach," Salmon says. "It chased me in here and wouldn't let me out. Wants us to stay in this stomach acid until we're digested."

He splashes at the water like it's no big deal.

"Stomach acid?" Tree examines the wall, stagger-slides through the water to it. He follows the corner, looking for something.

"What are you doing?" Salmon calls to him.

"There's got to be a way to cut ourselves out," Tree says through the gash in his neck.

"You can't cut through," Swan says from her island. "I've already tried."

"We've been eating the walls," Salmon says. "They aren't very good."

Tree returns to them. "Where did you cut?"

Swan points to the chewy holes behind her.

"It's too thick and it heals too quickly."

Tree tightens his vision…

"The acid," he says. "We can cut under the acid. It will slow the healing."

Tree splashes to a deep corner of the stomach and fires his blade deep into the underwater meat. The flesh shivers and rumbles around him. He pulls down, soaks himself up to his neck, and pushes his entire arm into the meat. Cutting, pushing his weight out to open the wound. He starts submerging his face to get down deeper. The water burns his eyes shut like concentrated chlorine.

A strip of light appears in the wound. The water level drops slightly, for just a moment.

"It's opened," Tree screams with acid like fire down his throat. "I see the other side."

Salmon swims over and nearly leaps onto Tree's back to look over his shoulder.

"Look at that!" he says.

The girl enters the pool and steps cautiously behind the men. Once she sees the light in the wound she pushes the men out of the way and hacks at the gash with her razor-clawed skeleton arm.

"Where do you think it goes?" Salmon asks.

"Who cares," Swan says. "Anywhere is better than here."

They cut into the wound and hold it open with their legs. Tree stretches as far down into the meat as he can reach and stomps at the sides until they snap wide.

The opening explodes beneath them and they find themselves riding a waterfall of spicy fluid out of the giant stomach and into midair. Free-falling.

They plop hard onto a metal platform. Acid dribbling onto their heads until the stomach's wound heals itself behind them.

Tree is getting choked to death. The spiky fish girl wrapped around him, hugging him with all her strength.

"Thank you, thank you!" she cries. "I love you!"

Her belly is firm but smooth against him. Not rough and spiky like the rest of her body. Snake belly textured. The seahorse-shaped features dig into Tree's neck, reopen the wound there.

Salmon is also hugging Tree, and hugging the girl, and hugging himself. He doesn't want to be left out.

Swan's underarms and inner thighs are as smooth as her belly as she cat-kisses Tree's cheek with her sticky iguana tongue. Then, without a blink, she lets him go and turns her back. More interested to see the outsides of the massive stomach above.

Salmon wonders how Tree will get around with one less foot.

They are standing on a large platform surrounded by walls of circuitry and electrical waterfalls. The flesh bag above is as big as a city, hanging by tendons from a ceiling too far away to see. Large veins crawling the sides of the stomach, pulsing, emitting watery digestive sounds and a smell like wet rat hair. There is nothing else organic about the scenery. It's all metal and electricity.

Swan goes to the edge of the platform and stops short.

Little Salmon follows her, licking his palms, but she waves him back.

"It's not flat," Swan says to Tree, tapping on the platform with her heel. "It's round."

Tree notices the curve in the distance. They're on top of some kind of giant metal sphere.

"What are we going to do?" Salmon asks.

"Keep ourselves from falling off," Swan says.

They spend the night on top of the sphere, not really sure what to do. Tree allowing his wounds to heal. His ankle has sealed up, rounded off on the end like a foot was never there.

Swan doesn't thank Tree anymore. She now blames him for trapping her on top of this enormous sphere and won't forgive him until he comes up with a plan to get them down. She allows Salmon to sit in her lap and sometimes bounces him on her knee like a baby or pretends to play drums with his arms. Salmon claps his hands with a big open smile.

Tree notices Swan has three extra shadows. Two men with curvy furniture bodies and a small teenaged girl with no hair. The girl's shadow seems ancient. Like the shadow of an Egyptian or tribal queen. They spread away from each other like they are desperate for privacy.

The little girl shadow on Tree is sneaking out from behind his legs to get a view of Swan's extra shadows. He almost forgot about her, his new dark side. He doesn't feel any different with her attached. He doesn't feel like she has influenced his behavior or made him a darker person. Swan has three extra shadows and according to Rowak that would make her a psychopathic demoness. But she doesn't seem that bad at all. Certainly not a threat to society. Perhaps she is just hiding her true personality or perhaps Rowak and CLOTTA don't know what they're talking about.

Tree examines his newfound shadow. She is probably ten years old, wearing a fluffy dress and pigtails. Tree wonders about her pigtails. Is she able to change her hairstyle? Does she need a shadow of a brush to manage her hair? How does she see the other shadows in her two-dimensional form? Perhaps the pigtails are pieces of meat growing out of her head like Swan's seahorse ridges.

When she notices Tree watching her, she darts back behind Tree's legs, safely hidden beneath (or within?) his shadow.

Swan and Salmon sleep curled together. Salmon almost half her size, coiled like a puppy in her spiky arms. The acid really dissolved him. If Tree hadn't come when he did Swan probably would have let him shrink to the size of a gerbil before letting him out of the digestive fluids.

Tree doesn't sleep. He watches the others, examining the details on the woman's skin, the vortex patterns and the bluish speckles on her neck. Her patterns are similar to Tree's. He has snail shell patterns and she has seahorse patterns. But her entire body is the texture of a seahorse and Tree is not the texture of a sea snail. She even has the same shaped skull as a seahorse. But with a very human face, freckled and hairless. With eyes like red fireworks within black marbles.

Tree counts her breaths. He watches the fluid trickling under the pale sections of her skin. For the most part, he remembers what humans are supposed to look like. How they looked on Earth. Staring at Swan's body he decides that this is better. They might no longer have sex organs, but now they are walking works of art.

CHAPTER SIX

The ground opens up and an elevator rises out of the sphere next to them. A man steps out. Very tall with coily blackish purple skin and a long blue beard. Wearing white shorts with a rope tied to his belt.

He sees Tree and snaps three fingers at him.

"There you are," the man says, pulling a clipboard out of his coat and handing it to Tree. "Sign here."

"What's this?" Tree asks.

The man creaks his head. "The work order…"

Tree shrugs.

"You're not the one who sent the work order?" he asks.

Blue Beard turns to see Swan and Salmon yawning and stretching awake.

"Wait a minute…" he says. "Who are you people?"

"Who are you?" Swan asks.

"There was supposed to be some kind of mess out here," says the man, twisting his beard. "I was assigned to clean it up. Boy are they going to be surprised when they find out the mess is a family of three."

He doesn't realize Salmon isn't ther child.

"Where did you come from anyway?" Blue Beard asks.

Tree points at the giant pulsating stomach sack.

The man's face scrunches into a ball. He whispers, "In there?"

Tree nods.

Blue Beard examines them. Notices the extra shadows, Tree's missing foot, Salmon's pink skin, the wound on the stomach where they emerged.

"You better come with me," he says, gently waving them over to the elevator.

Swan and Salmon help Tree onto his foot. He uses them as human crutches.

"Just don't let anyone see you," Blue Beard says.

Swan squeezes Tree's hand, excited and happy again.

There is another world within the sphere. A city is built around the inner walls and there is a small sun radiating from the center.

The elevator arrived into this world in a horizontal position. All four of them lying on their backs, piled together, staring up at the sun.

Salmon is blinded by the brightness, striking at it like wasps. "What is this place?"

"Heaven's Earth," Blue Beard says, poking a finger in and out of his belly button. "Gravity is reversed here. Instead of pulling toward the center it pushes outward."

Tree can't look at the sun for too long but Swan stares directly into it, completely mesmerized.

"I forgot all about the sun," she says. "How could I forget about something like that?"

Tree diverts his eyes and watches Blue Beard poke at his belly button. No, not a belly button. A hole. There are air holes running down his chest and belly. He sticks his fingers in and out of them like he is playing a flute.

They are inside of a small white room with a glass ceiling. It is wide open and clean with fresh lemon carpeting. The carpet fibers feel like plastic tattoos between Tree's fingers as they crawl out of the elevator and step outside onto the street.

Swan opens her arms to the warmth as Salmon and Tree examine the surroundings: it is a recreation of a 1950's suburban neighborhood, wrapped around the sun. Everything is overly colorful. Almost fake, as if they are within a giant model or children's playset. Everything made of plastic.

A car passes them on the road, slow and silent. It appears to be lightweight, without an engine. More like a windup toy than an automobile. Tree can't see the driver, but he feels as if he could lift the bright red car off the ground and tip it over if he wanted to.

"Cover your faces and don't speak to anyone," Blue Beard says. "Outsiders aren't allowed, for ecological reasons. Just follow me."

They follow Blue Beard through the neighborhood, past multi-colored people. Some wear fancy hats, sunglasses, scarves, but otherwise naked. Nobody pays attention to Tree hopping on one leg.

"We're trying to recapture the spirit of our past lives," Blue Beard says, leading them through the neighborhood. "We didn't know how to turn Heaven back into a paradise. The technology is too much for us to understand. But we learned enough to transform this tank into its own self-contained world based on memories we had of our past life. We created the happy American small town."

The farther they walk, the more artificial the buildings appear. It is hauntingly colorful. The homes around them seem so clean and perfect, as if nobody actually lives in them. Some doors and windows seem almost painted on the sides of the houses, as if they are just decoration and don't actually open.

"Not everyone here was from America," he continues. "Some weren't even from the era of automobiles and televisions. We do have televisions. There's only one channel but it's fun to watch. We have baseball, too."

"How do you remember what things used to be like?" Tree asks. "I don't remember anything."

"Memoria pills," Blue Beard says. "We have developed drugs that bring back memories."

"Can I get some?" Tree asks.

"Sure," he says.

"When? Soon?"

"Now, if you want. I always carry some around with me. Remembering is my favorite hobby. I used to be an astronaut." He digs into his pockets. "Here."

He drops five blue-egg pills into Tree's hand. "I can get you more later."

They arrive at a small house with a red fence and garden gnomes. Blue Beard opens the plastic gate and pets the gnomes.

"This is my second home," he says. "You can stay here for a while. Nobody will know you're here."

Swan is smiling, squeezing Tree's arm.

"I can't believe there's actually a civilization here," she whispers to Tree.

Blue Beard opens the front door. No lock. Takes them inside.

Swan says, "I've been looking for a place like this forever! Thank you!"

She is too excited to realize it... the difference.

After they enter the house, the colors disappear. Tree can feel it. He knows there's something wrong. The insides are not as colorful as the outside. It is gray and ashy within. The walls are cracked and blackened. Empty except for melting furniture and an old doll filled with beetle shells.

It feels like a tomb.

Blue Beard opens his mouth to say something to Swan but his voice is fading out. She can't understand him. He becomes transparent.

The window and the world outside of the door grows black. Blue Beard fractures into puzzle pieces and crumbles away. All that's left is a cold dead darkness watching them from outside.

Swan slams the door, gasping, leaning all of her weight against it so that nothing can get inside.

"What's wrong?" Tree asks. "What's happening?"

"It's happened to me before," Swan says. "In the old ruins."

"What?"

She shakes her head. "I don't know."

Salmon looks out of the window. The sun is burnt out. The houses in the neighborhood are dark and lifeless.

"This town is dead," Swan says. "Just like everything else in Heaven."

"But where is everyone?" Salmon asks.

"They were just ghosts," she says. "I knew it couldn't be for real."

Tree pulls her away from the door and hops outside, leans against the faded red fence. The buildings are now old and rotten. The grass is long dead. The pavement cracked. The sphere is even crumbling in on itself. A large hole has opened up on the east side and has taken out an entire block.

"It looks like it's been deserted for centuries," Tree says. "But it looks too modern to have been built centuries ago."

"Time is different in Heaven," Swan says. "For every year that passes on Earth, a hundred pass here. This place could have died five thousand years ago."

"So what do we do now?" Tree asks.

Swan kicks rubble across the yard.

"I think we should stay," Salmon says. "It's not so bad."

He sits down in a lawn chair, but it disintegrates under him.

Swan stares up at the dead sun. It is kind of like a moon now. It reflects the ghostly electric-blue light emanating from the hole in the sphere.

Tree still has the pills Blue Beard gave him.

"How is this possible?" he asks Swan, showing her the pills.

Swan just closes her eyes and plops her head onto his shoulder. Her nose rubbing against his sea snail skin.

Tree holds her and rubs his fingers along her spiny neck.

Tree and Swan take a walk through the cold ruins, the sidewalk cracking under their feet like sand dollars, Tree using Swan's shoulder like a crutch.

"I've been searching Heaven for years," Swan says, "trying to find evidence of God."

"No luck?"

"I'm convinced he is dead."

"CLOTTA and Rowak didn't say he was dead."

"They don't know. They like to think he is in one of the dead cities somewhere. Lingering. But they have never explored those cities. They have no proof."

"How do they know about the dead cities if they've never explored?"

"They don't. People have explored the dead cities ages ago, but that was long before CLOTTA came to Heaven. All those explorers are gone now. Died or disappeared in one way or another. But I've journeyed to those cities. A year ago I traveled from city to city. All of them the same. Rubble upon rubble. Like this place. Thousands of years dead. I eventually gave up and went back to CLOTTA's town. But unfortunately I was three shadows heavier and they sent me underground."

"You don't seem four times more evil than other people," Tree says.

"The number of shadows does not measure the evil of a person. CLOTTA's shadow is probably twice as evil as all six of our shadows put together. They are just lazy. They want to judge people in black and white. A person with more than one shadow is evil. A person with pink skin is annoying."

"A person with yellow skin is creative."

"Right. She isn't sure about any of it. She just makes assumptions. CLOTTA has only known a single yellow in the past. A girl who happened to be a good singer and dancer. Now she thinks all yellows will be wonderful singers. Same with pinks. Pinks aren't annoying people, they just happen to be a color that annoys CLOTTA."

"You don't seem to like her very much."

"You have no idea."

CHAPTER SEVEN

Squid-spiders ooze down the back of Tree's thigh.

"You're not sewn up," Swan says.

She takes him into a nearby ghost home, finds some needles and thread in a bathroom. The toilet is still intact. It is shaped like a cross between an Earth toilet and the toilet/buckets of Heaven.

Swan leans him against the wall and sews the lips of his ass together, wiping squid-spiders out of her way.

"Why are there bugs coming out of me?" Tree asks.

"It's the circle of life here," she says. "When you eat, your food gets recycled into new life. It might go in as cooked meats but comes out a colony of insects."

"That didn't happen before."

"It doesn't usually happen at first, but once your digestive system develops you'll be excreting all kinds of living things. It takes some getting used to."

"How long have you been in Heaven?"

"Not too long. Five years maybe. I still haven't gotten used to it. Everything here is as confusing now as it was the first week."

"Do you see any of the new colors? Have any new senses?"

"If I would have stayed with my mentor I would have known three new colors by now. He was training me to focus, to tap into the new senses, to explore the new limits of sight and taste and sound. But I wasn't a very good student."

Swan finishes stitching and bites the thread. "I'm still a baby, though. Just like you."

"What's the point?" Swan asks.

Tree, Salmon, and Swan are lying in the road, gazing up at

61

the other side of the city. The buildings like ugly clouds.

"The point of what?" Salmon asks.

"Continuing," she says. "God is dead. All the Heaven cities are dead. Not many people ever seem to cross anymore. And this is it. After we die here, we're gone forever."

"How do you know we die forever?" Salmon asks.

"Our souls are flesh now. Once our souls die, we die."

"Who says?" Salmon crosses his legs. "CLOTTA and Rowak are the ones who believe that. Who is to say we don't go to another afterlife after this one? And another one after that?"

Swan shakes her head.

"It's possible," Salmon says. "I didn't believe in Heaven and look at me now."

He turns to the yellow man. "What do you think, Tree?"

Tree croaks. "I don't even know if I believe we're really in Heaven at all."

"Why not?" Salmon uncrosses his legs.

"I don't know what Heaven is supposed to be like. I don't even know what I'm supposed to be like. I'm not sure of anything at all."

"Well, might as well just believe in whatever makes you happy," Salmon says. "Then at least you're happy until you're proven wrong."

Salmon rocks his head from side to side, lying between Tree and Swan with a big smile on his face.

Swan finds Tree an old foot in one of the abandoned houses.

"At least you'll be able to walk," she says.

The foot is more like a metal spider. Only there aren't any fangs. Swan clicks a lever on its side and it springs into life. The legs squirreling in the air at them.

"Here," she says.

The ball of the spider opens up to reveal a sparkling coil of bone that drills into the bottom of Tree's ankle. The pain is like bananas on the barbecue.

It locks into place. Tree's new foot is a collection of tiny metal insect legs.

"Try it out," Swan says.

Tree takes a step. The spider catches him. He doesn't feel the resistance of the ground, but his legs hold him up. It is awkward and unsteady.

"It'll work," Tree says. "I think."

Swan claps her hands and ripples her lips.

The spider foot bounces Tree's ankle up and down.

Tree puts the five pills on a concrete table that Salmon made out of the walls of another home. A fire burns in the corner of the room and emits rusty plum sensations.

"How should we split them?" Salmon asks.

"I don't want any," Swan says.

"Why not?"

"I don't trust them," she says. "Plus, I don't want to remember anyone I'm going to miss."

"I have to try," Tree says.

"You can have three," Salmon says to the yellow man. "Your memory is more important to you."

Salmon takes two of the pills and slips one in his mouth.

He almost instantly falls backward onto the floor and fades out of consciousness.

"Is he dead?" Tree asks.

"No," Swan says. "Sleeping."

Tree smiles at the spiky fish girl and kisses the blue pill before eating it. He is able to lie himself down before blacking out.

Tree is sucked back into his past. Into his old human skin. He understands the differences. The tightness of human flesh. The bland patternless skin. The itchiness. The clothes. The hair. The sweating. The testicles. All coming back to him.

His memory is in a hospital. He works here. He is a master surgeon. Maybe one of the best in the field. He doesn't know this for a fact, but he feels it, he sees it in the way people look at him as he walks through the halls. He is somebody important. He saves lives for a living. They all admire him.

He's an expert with a scalpel.

Tree, or whoever Tree used to be, enters an operating room with plump nurses and a birdy old man who waits quietly to be cut open by masterful hands. Surgeon Tree gets right to it. He doesn't need to concentrate. It is all casual. He slides rubber gloves onto his hands and whips a delicate blade off of a small metal table. And like an artist he flicks the knife into criss-crossy patterns lightning fast. Gashes open up on the patient before it even touches him.

With his precise incisions, he's able to take the old man apart into tiny pieces and then reassemble him into something better. Something that works correctly. His hands move faster than the eyes can see, but Surgeon Tree doesn't need to look at what he's doing. He just stares straight ahead, over the bulbous nurses' shoulders. Checking time on the clock and counting tiles in the ceiling.

As Tree's mechanical limbs tornado blood into the air, causing a wind that curls the old man's tongue to the back of his wide-open mouth, the nurses burst into a thundering of applause and nod their heads with utmost respect.

Tree awakes to Salmon leaning over him, jerking him out of his memory.

"What? What?" Tree cries.

"Do you remember?" Salmon asks.

Salmon scrunches Tree's yellow chest skin.

"Do I remember what?" Tree smacks his little hands away,

and looks around for Swan but she is not in the room.

"Us," Salmon says.

"You interrupted my memory," Tree says. "I was enjoying it."

"What was your memory? Was I in it?"

"No. I was at work. At a hospital. I was a famous surgeon on Earth. I think..."

"Then you don't know?"

"Know what?"

"We were..."

"Yeah?"

"Lovers," Salmon whispers. "We were married."

"Married? Were you a woman on Earth?"

"No, we are gay. You love me. Don't you remember?"

"I don't remember anything about being gay."

"But you *are* gay. You're my husband." Salmon lays his face across Tree's chest.

Tree pushes him and backs away.

"We're soul mates," Salmon says. "That's why we arrived in Heaven at the same time. We're destined to be together forever."

"I don't believe it," Tree says. "I'm not in the least bit attracted to you."

"You just don't remember me. I felt the same way when my mind was blank." Salmon grabs a pill from the table. "Here, take another pill. You'll remember me."

Salmon tries to pry open Tree's mouth but Tree pushes him back.

"Get away from me."

Tree exits the rotten house and runs into the moldy streets.

CHAPTER EIGHT

Tree wanders through the gray ruins of city, past cars melted into the ground, past mailboxes filled with dust.

He can hear Salmon calling out for him, so he walks in the opposite direction of the voice.

It must be a lie. How could Salmon recognize him in his Earth skin? He must be confused. It must be another man from his past that is somewhat similar to Tree. In Salmon's case Swan was right. It is a horrible thing to remember somebody you will miss. Perhaps he misses his lover so much that he has convinced himself that Tree is his husband in a new form.

Tree heads downtown. He wants to get the pink man out of his head so he can concentrate on his new memory.

A surgeon...

He must have been a brilliant man.

"Give me a hand," Swan says from behind a building downtown.

Tree didn't realize she was out this far. In the urban section full of micro skyscrapers and trolley tracks. It doesn't look very safe here, ready to collapse on them at any moment.

Swan is carrying crates into a grocery cart. Full of jars and cans of food.

"There's some kind of shelter down there," she says. "Most of the food seems well preserved."

Tree looks through the provisions. They are packaged like food from Earth. Even labeled with commercial logos. But most of the food is unfamiliar. He doesn't understand the writing, but there are pictures of blue and red eel-turtles on some of the cans. And pictures of thorny potato juice on others.

"What do you think happened to them?" Tree asks.

"Died out, I guess," she says. "Like everyone else in Heaven."

"Do you really think we're the only ones left in Heaven?" Tree asks.

"Besides CLOTTA's community, and the creatures who live on the landscape, yeah. I think we're all alone."

Tree brushes concrete powder off of Swan's shoulder and then helps her load the crates.

Tree and Swan in the underground subway system, sitting in the crusty seats of an old subway car, eating pickled lobster-apples and kicking their legs around.

"So what did the pill teach you?" Swan asks.

"I used to be a doctor," Tree says. "A specialist."

"Good for you," she says, as if she's annoyed that he remembered something about himself.

"I bet people used to travel all over the world just to receive treatment from me. There must have been procedures that only I could perform properly."

"You must have been rich," she says.

"I don't remember being rich yet. Just gifted."

"What about Salmon? What did he used to be?"

Tree cringes. "He didn't say."

"He didn't tell you his memory?" she asks.

"Well, he said that we knew each other in our past lives."

"Really?"

"He said we were lovers. Maybe even married."

Swan laughs. "You were homosexual?"

"I don't know. He says so. I don't believe him."

"Why don't you believe him?"

"It's impossible. I'm not attracted to him."

"He looks different now. Perhaps you'd find his human form attractive."

"I don't know if I was gay on Earth, but I'm definitely not gay now."

"Why's that?"

"Because I'm attracted to you."

Swan smirks. "So I've noticed."

"You've noticed?" Tree asks.

"I can sense these things," Swan says. "It's not really a new sense, more like an extension of sight, but I'm able to see the emotions coming out of you. It's something that develops naturally your first year in Heaven."

Tree blushes.

"Don't be ashamed," Swan says. "It's beautiful, the way you feel about me. A bit sudden for such a strong feeling, but I like the way it dances out of your flesh. Like sun-peaches and pools of mercury swimming through the air."

Tree watches her follow invisible streams in the air. Her sparkler eyes capturing him inside of them.

She giggles. "Now you're getting aroused."

"Aroused?" he asks. "How can I be aroused? We can't have sex in Heaven. We don't have the parts."

"What are you talking about?" Swan says. "Of course we can still have sex in Heaven."

"How?" Tree asks.

"CLOTTA didn't take you to her bed?"

"No."

"She usually sleeps with all the newcomers."

"I was only there for a day."

"Well, then I'll have to show you how it's done," she says.

Swan arches her back to shove her spiky breasts into his face. A grin stretches across her swamp-green lips like she's about to corrupt the innocent and the idea is issuing clouds of molten violet glass from pores on her skin.

Tree has no idea what to do. He doesn't really remember having sex as a human. He just remembers it required a penis and an orifice to put it in.

He tries to follow her lead. She kisses him, sucks his golden lips into her mouth. Her tongue goos out onto his shoulder. Tree looks into her mouth. She's toothless. There are ridges of cartilage but it's more fish-like than human. Her entire mouth is a stretching of tongue that rolls out of her lips and massages the back of Tree's neck.

She smiles excitedly at Tree's millipede tongue. Its hundreds of legs are more like thin tentacles. They run across Swan's cheek and tickle her ear.

Swan presses her lips against the millipede and closes her eyes. As her giant tongue slides into Tree's mouth, she begins to shiver. It slips down into his throat and back into his mouth.

She pushes away from him and looks deep into his eyes.

"You like that?" she asks.

Tree nods.

She sticks her tongue back into his mouth and shoves it further down his throat this time. He can feel it tickle the insides of his chest. He tastes rust-fuzzy.

She begins fucking his throat with her tongue. Throat sensations like a vagina, but more intense, his nerves in a complex web of sensuality. Tree attempts to put his tongue into her throat but is overpowered by the seahorse girl's massive shaft of meat. He wonders if her tongue will cum inside him like a penis.

Swan throws Tree onto the floor of the subway car. Her tongue flaps at him like a nervous tail. Before Tree realizes what is happening, the green girl pulls his blade out of his arm and cuts his belly open from his crotch to his ribcage. Tree gasps in shock as she straddles his thighs. Her lips puffed at him, eyes glowing into him as she spreads open the new lips on his torso and slides her fingers inside.

Tree explodes with new sensations as she explores his goopy insides with worming fingers. Orange mucus pours out of Tree like globs of blood. She seizes something inside of him, up inside of his chest that makes his entire body ache and squirm.

She pulls on it, slips it out of his torso and shows it to him. The organ is as large as a lung but pulses like a heart. It reminds Tree of a water balloon made from a doctor's rubber glove, with several thick white tubes that connect it to the inside of his chest.

Swan opens her mouth around the organ and sucks one of its wriggling udders. Tree's limbs soothe into calm. It feels like his entire body is inside of her mouth. The iguana tongue oozes out of her deep green lips and coils around the pulsing organ. Bloody nuggets dripping out of the sides, clinging between her fingers and taste-buds.

Then Swan's breathing becomes rapid. She licks the orange goop from Tree's knife and quickly cuts into her own belly, impatiently, sloppily. She groans as she squeezes out an identical meat-balloon from inside of her, behind her spiky breasts and holds it up. She pauses. One organ in each hand. Holds her breath. Mouth wide open and tongue dangling out as she slowly presses them together.

Tree sees the fingers of the organs curl around each other and then blank. Sensual overload. His sight becomes all white, all sound disappears, smells erased. All he can feel is a cosmic squishing of his soul-flesh into Swan's. His entire body melting into her, rubbing against every molecule of her being. Endlessly orgasming.

They are swallowed by each other. Digesting one another.

For a moment, they do merge completely. Become one consciousness. Tree forgets which soul is his, which particles are his, which thoughts.

He is the closest he's ever been to anyone, even himself.

Tree awakes wet and bristly in the subway car. His head in Swan's breasts. Though spiky, her chest is surprisingly comfortable. Their bellies still open, spilling fizzy fluids onto the floor. But Swan has put the sex organs back into their original containers.

"What happened?" he asks.

"You blacked out just before we climaxed." She wipes grease from his forehead. "I was expecting you to. Nobody makes it to climax their first time. Especially someone so young."

"You didn't tell me it was like that," Tree says.

"No, I guess I didn't," she says, big green smile.

"How many times have you done it?"

"Dozens," she says. "Mostly with CLOTTA. She was the best. The older souls can do amazing things. I can't even begin to explain it. This was the first time I was the leader. It was pretty fun. You should try it with Salmon sometime."

Tree shakes his head. "I don't think so."

"You might someday remember loving him," Swan says.

"If I do it won't change anything. That was another life. I'm a different person now."

"We'll see," Swan says.

A snake of pudding slimes out of her belly and down Tree's back.

From the back of the subway, Salmon watches Tree and Swan lying together, bellies open at each other. He grips a fire axe in his hand, twisting his palms against it. A corner of the axe blade stabs into his pink thigh. It eases only a little of his pain.

Tree and Swan push withered old grocery carts full of supplies down the suburban sidewalk. The carts are ready to fold inward, wheels ready to break apart, and the sidewalk is too rough and rocky, but they try to get as far as possible before abandoning the carts.

"We can probably stay here for quite a while with all this stuff," Swan says.

"Yeah, I'd like that," Tree says.

They smile at each other. Their eyes glowing in the dimness.

Their bellies are sewn up with fresh thread. Swan found everything they'll need in the shelter under the city. She even found extra knives for cutting their stomachs open again.

They find a new home. A sturdyish one on a better preserved side of town. There is even a place for them to sleep, an old mattress that has withered down to a pile of soft stuffing.

Cuddling together on the musty mound, Swan drops deep into sleep within Tree's arms. He just about falls asleep against her when a shadowy form jerks him awake.

"Take it," Salmon says.

He leans over the bed, a little boy with an axe, his fist stretched to Tree.

"What are you doing in here?" Tree asks, then he notices the axe.

"I don't want to hurt you," Salmon says. "But I'm going to split your skull in half if you don't take this pill."

"That was another life," Tree says. "Even if I was your lover on Earth, I won't be in Heaven. I'm a different person now."

"I just want you to remember what I remember," Salmon says. "The two of us were happy together. In love. If you can just remember, I'll be satisfied. Even if you don't want to be with me."

"I don't trust you," Tree says. "Why do you have that axe?"

"I promise I won't hurt you if you take the pill," Salmon says.

"I'll be unconscious. If you hurt her while I'm out I will slice you to shreds."

"I don't want to hurt anybody. I just want you to take the pill."

He drops it on Tree's chest.

"I'm serious," Tree says. "I'll cut you to pieces."

He slips the pill into Tree's mouth.

As Salmon sets down the axe, Tree swallows.

Salmon watches his face excitedly as he fades out.

Tree bursts out of the bed at Salmon. His knife whips out of his arm and presses against the pink man's thin neck.

Salmon screams, Swan jerks awake.

"What's going on?" Swan cries.

"You promised you'd take the pill," Salmon whines.

"Shut up!" Tree says.

"You promised!"

"You son of a bitch!" Tree says.

"I just wanted you to remember…"

"You fucking piece of shit!" Tree says.

"Why didn't you just take it?" Salmon says. "That's all I wanted."

"I did take it."

"Really? Did you remember? How we were?"

"You killed us, you sick fuck!" Tree says.

"What?" Salmon cries.

Swan keeps her distance.

"You selfish prick! You killed us both!"

Tree knees the little man in the stomach and throws him out of the room.

"Stay away from me," Tree says.

Salmon's face droops at the yellow man.

"Go!" Tree screams.

Salmon runs out of the house and down the street.

He keeps running, around the globe of the city, and then around it again. He keeps running until his legs can no longer move. Then he finds a dark room to collapse in. He crawls into a corner, curls into a ball, and bites his knees. Streams of tears soaking his salmon-colored skin.

CHAPTER NINE

Tree is shitting copper spring worms in the black-fuzzy bathroom.

"Can you tell me now?" Swan asks, helping him balance on his new spider/foot.

He wants to be alone, but he knows he can't sew himself up all by himself. Swan bends over and stabs the needle into his hind flesh.

"I can see your emotions," she says. "Don't bother trying to hide them."

"He was right," Tree says. "We were lovers. At one time."

"So you were gay?" she teases.

Tree smacks her forehead with his butt for saying that, the needle poking her fingertip.

"It wasn't quite like that," he says. "I didn't think in terms of male and female, gay and straight, when I was on Earth. I just needed to be close to someone. Anyone. I didn't care what their gender was. I was attracted to the affection."

"You weren't in love with him?"

"Perhaps I was on some level, but I was just with him because it was comfortable and convenient."

Swan bites the thread and lets Tree go.

"One day I found somebody else and was ready to move on. It was a normal cycle for me. I would stay with one person until I found somebody new. Then I'd move on. This time it was a woman. A painter. She was a neighbor and I could tell she wanted to try a relationship with me. I could always tell. Salmon couldn't handle it though. He couldn't let me go. He threatened to kill himself. On the ledge of my apartment building. I tried to stop him. I don't know why. I didn't love him anymore. It would have been an easy way to get him out of my life forever. But he didn't want to be saved. He just wanted me to get close enough to him so he could grab me and take me with him. He killed us. I was such an important person. My skills as a surgeon were incomparable. But he killed me. For such a stupid reason."

"It doesn't sound like a stupid reason to me," she says. "He loved you."

"It wasn't love. It was something sick."

Days pass.

Swan and Tree have cleaned out the house and converted it into a comfortable home. It is swarming with crawly creatures from their excrement. Snail-bats, monkey-lizards, troll-mice. Swan pretends they are all their children and keeps them as pets. Tree doesn't seem to mind them so much.

They haven't seen Salmon since the fire axe incident. He just disappeared into the ruins and became a wandering ghost. A lost soul. Sometimes they hear a distant voice in the night and assume that it is him.

Their sex is getting better, but Tree still can't make it all the way to the climax. His senses don't overload as easily though.

Most of their days are spent in bed, holding each other, content with their eternity. But sometimes they go out and explore the old ruins. There's a dead park where they go on picnics. A merry-go-round that still works. Many interesting places where they can have sex.

It's not quite Heaven, but it's good enough.

An earthquake hits one morning. A very small tremor but it causes the crack in the sphere to widen. Several large buildings collapse downtown. Thick clouds of dust fill the air like smog.

"I don't like it," Swan says.

"It wasn't that bad," Tree says.

75

"It was bad enough," she says. "We're not safe here."

Swan and Tree spend the day looking for a way out. The elevator they entered the town with is no longer operating.

"We're trapped," Tree says.

"No, there's got to be another way."

They continue hunting. The town is mostly rubble. If there are any exits they've all been buried a long time ago.

"Maybe we can see something from the other side of the sphere," Tree says. "By looking through the fissure."

Swan nods.

Another minor earthquake as they get close to the crack in the sphere. The fissure is acting like a fault line. The sides pressured outward with the artificial gravity, rubbing the edges together to create a rumble through the entire city.

"It's unstable," Swan says. "It can collapse at any time."

The streets near the cracking fissure are weak. They break apart like thin ice.

Swan stops Tree. "Wait."

She uses Tree's knife to cut a slit in her hip and with two fingers she pulls a meaty cord out of her side.

She stretches it, coils it like a lasso.

"Here," she says.

She ties the tendon around Tree's waist. Then pulls more of the string out of her torso for slack.

"Do you remember mountain climbing?" she asks.

Tree shakes his head.

"I'm going to be your safety," she says. "You'll lean outside of the sphere and have a look around."

"Shouldn't you be doing this?" he asks, feeling Swan's warm fluids pumping through the meat rope around his waist. "Your vision is stronger than mine."

Swan taps her nose. "You'll be fine."

Tree walks across the crackling asphalt toward the opening in the ground. He can see the overwhelming Heaven-circuitry and electric waterfalls on the other side. It occurs to him that they might just be decorative. Everything unfamiliar doesn't always have to have a function.

He looks back at Swan. She smiles, feeding him more slack from her goopy insides.

Before Tree gets a chance to look away from Swan, the ground breaks apart underneath him and he drops down into empty space.

Tree doesn't fall far. His body flaps out into space for just a moment before it rolls backward onto the outside of the sphere.

He lies there for a moment, staring out at the electric waterfalls. Then he rolls over on his belly, crawls to the fissure, and peeks back through the hole to see an upside-down Swan trying to reel in her belly cord.

"I'm okay," he says.

Her mouth wide open.

"There's gravity out here. I'll have a look around."

Swan nods slowly and feeds him more of the tendon.

Tree stands himself, his spider foot scrambles to find balance. The sphere is in the center of another giant sphere. He can't tell the distance to the walls of the outer sphere, but he can tell they are very far. It is like they are on the inside of a planet.

There is a small cement building on the other side of the fissure.

A face is staring out of the window at him. A pink face.

Tree circles around the hole, careful not to cut Swan's flesh string, just now realizing that her nerves must stretch all the way up the cord.

"I would never hurt you," Salmon says to Tree from the window.

"What are you doing out here?" Tree asks.

"I tried to jump," he says.

Tree approaches the small building. It is the size of a bathroom.

"I didn't really kill us, did I?" Salmon asks.

"You couldn't accept that I didn't want to be with you anymore," Tree says.

"I must have gone crazy," he says. "I couldn't imagine living without you."

"We shouldn't have taken those pills," Tree says. "Things were better before."

"Maybe. But our memories made us who we are. Without them we were lost."

"I think CLOTTA was right. We're better off forgetting about our past for now. We need to move forward."

"I already took another pill. I saw when we first met. You killed a man for me. You killed a skinhead bouncer. Behind a pub. You cut his neck open with your scalpel.

"You sliced him up in such an artistic and beautiful way. Like you were dancing tango with him instead of slaughtering him. After it was all over and you dabbed up droplets of blood from your neck, you told me that you did it for me. We were strangers. It was the first time I ever saw you and you killed a man for me. It was love at first sight."

"I'm sorry," Tree says. "I don't remember. I don't want to remember anymore. That person is no longer who I am."

Salmon lowers his head.

"We're trying to find a way out of here," Tree says. "If we find a way you can come with us. But I don't want to hear about our past lives. That is ancient history. Understand?"

Salmon is red-faced at him.

Tree steps away from the pink man's shelter and examines

the exterior of the sphere.

Another small earthquake.

Tree's spider foot squirms in different directions, throwing him off balance but he does not fall.

When it is over, Salmon appears at Tree's legs. "I think I know a way out."

Tree kneels down.

"I haven't tried it yet," says the child-sized man, "but I think it'll work."

Tree helps Swan crawl out of the city and onto the shell of the sphere. Once she is on the exterior, Tree unties her flesh rope from his waist and coils it up for her. She stuffs it back inside of her with a twist of her hips.

"Over here," Salmon says. He leads them across the metal surface to a large plastic tube stretching out of the sphere and up into the abyss of Heaven's circuits. The tube contains a cart. It looks like it was made for cargo, not passengers. For shooting supplies from one end of Heaven to the other.

"It's worth trying," Tree says.

Swan shakes her spiky head at him.

It takes several hours, or what seems like hours, for Swan to figure a way to power up the cart. Tree wants to help but he doesn't remember the mechanics of earthly machines let alone Heavenly ones, so he watches Salmon do solemn cartwheels along the metal surface.

When Swan gets it going, she has no idea how she did it. Some fidgeting in the right places did the trick.

She says, "It's kind of like a vacuum tube mixed with a hot air balloon."

Swan pulls a lever from outside and they hurry within the

cart, hold tightly to each other, then they blast off.

The blast causes another earthquake, a larger one. They can see the sphere crumble in on itself in another section, but it doesn't yet go to pieces. Holding itself together by threads.

"It won't be there much longer," Swan says. "We're lucky to get out when we did."

"We should have taken the rest of our supplies," Tree says. "We don't know where we'll end up."

The spiky fish girl holds his hand as they glide through space. The tube splits off in several directions every hundred feet. But they don't have control over their destination. Swan really didn't have a clue what she was doing.

CHAPTER TEN

They arrive in a landscape of black melty razor glass bushes. It could be the same landscape Tree arrived in when he came to Heaven.

"No, it's different," Salmon says, pointing to the hills. The grass is white with a layer of snow or cotton or, as Salmon describes it, marshmallow sauce.

There are also large mushroom-like trees that look like oozing turtle pies. The sky is the same green as it was. Kind of like the color of Swan's lips. But now with hook-shaped clouds spilling in like ocean breakers.

"It's good to be above ground," Swan says.

Tree frowns at her and the landscape.

Salmon picks bone-figs out of murk trees.

"Hey look, we have food," he shouts. "These are good." He bites into one and scrunches his face at the bitter fruit.

The spiky fish girl sway-walks over to him and examines them.

"Those are poisonous," she says, then laughs at him.

"No they're not," Salmon says with a fig dangling from his mouth. "I eat them all the time."

Swan picks him out of the tree and gives him a piggy-back ride, bone-figs raining down her back as she runs in circles around the bushes.

Tree scans the surroundings. No signs of civilization. Maybe over the white hills.

He hikes toward a hill of snowy grass. Swan and her screaming passenger race through the turtle-shaped mushrooms to catch up to him.

On top of the hill, they see a city in the far distance. There aren't any roads so they follow the fields of white, making it easier to spot any shadows that might try creeping up on them.

The closer they get to the city the larger it appears.

"I've never been to this one before," Swan says. "It's enormous. A kingdom."

Salmon spots a road from the green girl's shoulders. The road is mostly piles of large flat stones that disappear into the white grass hill. It doesn't look like it's been used in a very long time.

"Another dead one," Swan says.

"You don't know," Salmon says. "It's a huge city. People might live on the other side."

There doesn't appear to be any movement within the city at all, but Tree feels like he is being watched.

The buildings are like Roman palaces built for the Titans. Salmon especially feels small walking through the streets.

"This is the oldest city I've seen," Swan says. "The Greek Gods must have lived here."

"Were the Greek Gods real?" Salmon asks.

"Probably not," Swan says. "But you never know. The old ones were giants like the Greek Gods. We really don't know anything about them. They left some homes and furniture behind. That's the only proof we have that they were ever here."

Their steps echo softly through the whispering houses. The street as wide as a field. Salmon makes them hold his hands as they walk through the ancient ghost town.

"This was a major city," Swan says. "Maybe it's the city where God lived."

Searching the metropolis. The buildings are all empty. No furniture or belongings left behind. Just the occasional cobweb or pile of leaves. The farther into the city they go, the larger the buildings become. Even larger giants lived out here.

Swan finds a family of angels living in a garden in a rural section of town.

"There is life here," she says.

The masturbating babies flap through the fruit trees and duck into bushes.

"Do you think they're the only ones here?" Salmon asks.

"Can't be," Swan says. "Angels don't have the intelligence to tend a garden properly. Somebody must look after them."

There are no signs of life except for the small garden of angels. Sometimes golf-birds will fly out of windows across the street, but it is otherwise dead.

"Why do I feel like we're being followed?" Tree asks. "Watched?"

"I have that feeling too," Salmon says.

"It's normal." Swan glances into the giant windows and doors around them. "These deserted cities always give you that feeling."

The buildings stare down on them with angry eyebrows.

Where the buildings stretch higher than mountains, they find the center of the city. A castle. The tallest and grandest structure they've ever seen in Heaven. It bursts into their view with brilliance and thousands of overwhelming colors.

"Look at it," Swan says. "That has to be the house of God."

The structure is more alive than any other building in the city. It is crawling with vegetation. Vines like centipedes of purple human hands coat a large section of the building. From between the massive bricks grow dog-sized flowers that are an icy moon color Tree has never seen before. Stick-birds circle the tower high above. Cat-hoppers watch them with sharp snail eyes.

They approach the gate of the castle. The bars have fused shut over time. Razor-vines thick as oak trees slither up the iron bars.

"We're like bugs," Salmon says, as they crawl under the gate. "Like cockroach people invading a home."

They step into the courtyard. An entire landscape in itself. Forests of silver trees and black rose bushes stretch across God's lawn.

Swan can spot ledges in the massive front door where trees have sprouted. Caves have cracked open to support wasp-eagle nests.

"I'm beginning to think CLOTTA was right," Swan says. "She always said that God still lives in the deserted ruins of the capital city. All alone in his giant castle that's higher than the clouds. She never saw it for herself, so I didn't believe her. But this could be it."

"He might be on his deathbed," Tree says. "Not quite dead yet, but pretty much on his last breaths."

The cockroach people stare up at the door like a cliff and wonder how they're ever going to get it open.

There isn't any space between the ground and the door for them to crawl under. The door doesn't seem to have been opened in thousands of years. It is grown into the ground, become a part of the doorframe. No cracks or holes. Completely blocked.

They follow the wall, searching for some kind of opening.

"CLOTTA said it's forbidden to come here," Tree says. "They wouldn't make it easy to get in if it's forbidden."

"They also wouldn't leave it unguarded," Swan says.

They have lunch in an apple grove that grows cheesesteak flavored apples, resting in blue mushroom grass and staring up at the beastly structure. Just waiting for some sign of life to show itself.

Swan takes a nap under some shade as the two men go for a walk.

"I want to learn how they used to cut shadows off," Salmon says.

"Why do that?" Tree asks.

"So that I don't have to love you anymore," he says.

"Cutting your shadow off is going to change that?"

"On Earth, priests said that homosexuality is evil," Salmon says. "If it's evil then it's a part of my shadow and I can cut it off of me. I wouldn't have to love you or any other man ever again."

"What if homosexuality isn't evil?" Tree asks.

"The priests said it was."

"The priests were wrong about a lot of things."

Tree is squatting behind an apple tree, trying to excrete his recycled lunch.

He's facing his shadow, examining it. There isn't a sun so he doesn't know what light source is creating it. Perhaps it is God Himself. The castle is directly behind him. Perhaps the shadows in Heaven always point away from God, hiding from Him.

The little girl shadow stands up from behind his true shadow and waves. She still has a mind of her own, but normally likes to blend into the other shadow. It is her protection blanket. The girl moves her limbs at Tree, as if trying to communicate.

This is the first time the yellow man has had constipation in Heaven. He really feels like he has to go but nothing is coming out.

The little girl's shadow makes finger puppets for him. She does a dog and a duck pretty well. He laughs out loud at each one to be polite, but he doesn't really know how to act around kids. He's not even sure if she can hear or see him.

In his shadow, Tree notices something odd is coming out of him. There is an extra hand in the shadow and it isn't one of his or the little girl's. He stretches his head until he can see between his legs.

He is excreting a human hand.

It looks like it is growing out of his homemade rectum, fingers wiggling at him, and he opens his mouth to scream but Salmon and Swan scream for him instead.

Something is trying to kill them.

The black rose bushes are too thick for Tree to see what's going on, but there is something chasing after his friends.

The keen blade flips out of Tree as quick as a switchblade. When he tries to run, he is thrown backward. The hand growing out of his rear has grabbed hold of a tree root.

The yellow man pulls at the hand, tries to pry open its fingers but it won't budge.

He can see the danger now. Goblin-octopus creatures are driving his friends away from the grove. There are dozens of them. Salmon screeches like a banshee at them, and they shriek back at him in an even higher pitch.

Tree squats down and positions his feet as close to the hand as possible. Then shoves off.

He can feel the rectum gash rip higher up his back. Then POP and he flies into the dirt.

Looking back: a human head lies on the ground before him. A living bodiless head with an arm attached to the front of its face like an elephant's trunk. Its fingers still clutching the apple tree's root. Its eyeballs blinking and rolling around in their sockets.

Tree chases after the horde of octopus creatures as they circle the castle wall. They have long chain-link tentacles and a blender of metal teeth.

He doesn't need to think about his actions. They all come naturally to him. The blade cuts their legs out from under them as he passes through the horde, removes their teethy heads from their necks.

White fluid like blood sprays out of their missing limbs and coats his face, almost blinding him.

Leaving a trail of thrashing bleeding bodies all the way to the back of the castle where he catches up to the bulk of the group, crowded around a vined wall.

Swan and Salmon are up in the purple millipede vines, dodging the chain tentacles. Salmon doesn't look conscious. His body limp. A large gash across his chest and insect sludge dumping out of him.

The seahorse girl can't climb any higher. She uses all of her strength to keep Salmon from falling.

Tree cuts a row of them down before the mob realizes he is there. They turn to him and shiver their tentacles at him violently. One of them hooks his leg with a barbed chain from behind, but Tree de-throats the shrieker before it can fling him away from the crowd.

Wave after wave, the metal octopus soldiers charge at him with slashing chain tentacles, but Tree is too fast for them. His arm tornados, dodging their limbs and striking vital organs. He mows them down like grass, climbing up their milky corpses.

His spider foot launches him high over the crowd and catches a vine with its metal legs. It crawls up the vine for Tree, strong enough to pull his whole body up as he hangs upside-down slashing at the creatures without even looking in their general direction.

They do not climb the vines after him. They just glare at him, blender-teeth roaring and grinding with anger.

Tree sees Swan staring down at him from a wide ledge above.

"You're amazing with that," she says, helping him onto the balcony.

"It is a part of me," Tree says.

They are on some kind of windowsill garden. A field of vast food trees and ponds. Tree steps down into the soil next to Salmon's body.

"Is he dead?" Tree asks.

"I think he'll make it," Swan says. "We'll see in the morning."

Tree is on the edge of the balcony, gazing out at Heaven's vast landscape. He can see the ocean from here, just past the city limits. A great green ocean stretching out to the horizon.

He wonders if there are islands out there. Or other continents. Heaven is probably a thousand times the size of Earth. Limitless. Full of lands for them to explore.

Swan is eating piles and piles of fruit. She says they are the most amazing things she's ever tasted. After an hour her stomach balloons out like a puffer fish.

"You look pregnant," Tree says.

"Maybe I am," she says.

"Is that possible here?" he asks.

"No," she says. "But who knows, maybe the food will be recycled into a baby."

She rolls her swollen belly at him, imagining a yellow spiky baby inside her. Tree doesn't want to think about it. It reminds him of the human head with an arm for a snout that came out of him earlier.

"I don't doubt the possibility," Tree says.

The sky is darkening to a navy blue. Tree and Swan huddle together, watching the ocean in the distance.

"Have you looked through the window yet?" Tree asks.

Swan doesn't answer the question.

She is distant. Eyes soaking in the atmosphere.

"It's nice here," Swan says. "I think we should stay for a while. We can build a house by the lake. Grow vegetables in the garden."

"I thought you wanted to see if God really exists?" Tree asks, rubbing her ribbed thigh.

Swan shrugs.

She closes her eyes and breathes deeply, absorbing the fresh sunny-flavored air.

The spiky fish girl sleeps in Tree's lap, drooling down his yellow skin. Salmon lies in a cozy hole in the soil. Maybe alive, maybe dead.

Tree looks back and forth between the ocean and the enormous window behind them. A faint blue light emanates from somewhere beyond the edge of the frame. There's nothing else he can see on the other side. Just a haunting blue glow.

There are giant beasts out in the sea that will occasionally surface for air. Whale-like creatures made of hundreds of hairy elephants melted together. Eyes like freckles on the sides of their lobster heads.

They sing to Tree in warm glassy voices. A lullaby with lyrics he can't possibly understand. But he enjoys the soothing sensations that caress in and out of the back of his neck as he listens to them, weakening his eyes, drawing him closer and closer to sleep, as he peers out across the vast landscape of Heaven.

An infant peering out over its crib.

ABOUT THE AUTHOR

Carlton Mellick III is one of the leading authors of the bizarro fiction subgenre. Since 2001, his books have drawn an international cult following, despite the fact that they have been shunned by most libraries and chain bookstores.

He won the Wonderland Book Award for his novel, *Warrior Wolf Women of the Wasteland*, in 2009. His short fiction has appeared in *Vice Magazine, The Year's Best Fantasy and Horror #16, The Magazine of Bizarro Fiction,* and *Zombies: Encounters with the Hungry Dead*, among others. He is also a graduate of Clarion West, where he studied under the likes of Chuck Palahniuk, Connie Willis, and Cory Doctorow.

He lives in Portland, OR, the bizarro fiction mecca.

Visit him online at **www.carltonmellick.com**

BIZARRO BOOKS

CATALOG   FALL 2011

ERASERHEAD PRESS

Your major resource for the bizarro fiction genre:

WWW.BIZARROCENTRAL.COM

Introduce yourselves to the bizarro fiction genre and all of its authors with the Bizarro Starter Kit series. Each volume features short novels and short stories by ten of the leading bizarro authors, designed to give you a perfect sampling of the genre for only $10.

BB-0X1
"The Bizarro Starter Kit"
(Orange)
Featuring D. Harlan Wilson, Carlton Mellick III, Jeremy Robert Johnson, Kevin L Donihe, Gina Ranalli, Andre Duza, Vincent W. Sakowski, Steve Beard, John Edward Lawson, and Bruce Taylor. **236 pages $10**

BB-0X2
"The Bizarro Starter Kit"
(Blue)
Featuring Ray Fracalossy, Jeremy C. Shipp, Jordan Krall, Mykle Hansen, Andersen Prunty, Eckhard Gerdes, Bradley Sands, Steve Aylett, Christian TeBordo, and Tony Rauch. **244 pages $10**

BB-0X2
"The Bizarro Starter Kit"
(Purple)
Featuring Russell Edson, Athena Villaverde, David Agranoff, Matthew Revert, Andrew Goldfarb, Jeff Burk, Garrett Cook, Kris Saknussemm, Cody Goodfellow, and Cameron Pierce **264 pages $10**

BB-001 **"The Kafka Effekt" D. Harlan Wilson** — A collection of forty-four irreal short stories loosely written in the vein of Franz Kafka, with more than a pinch of William S. Burroughs sprinkled on top. **211 pages $14**

BB-002 **"Satan Burger" Carlton Mellick III** — The cult novel that put Carlton Mellick III on the map ... Six punks get jobs at a fast food restaurant owned by the devil in a city violently overpopulated by surreal alien cultures. **236 pages $14**

BB-003 **"Some Things Are Better Left Unplugged" Vincent Sakwoski** — Join The Man and his Nemesis, the obese tabby, for a nightmare roller coaster ride into this postmodern fantasy. **152 pages $10**

BB-004 **"Shall We Gather At the Garden?" Kevin L Donihe** — Donihe's Debut novel. Midgets take over the world, The Church of Lionel Richie vs. The Church of the Byrds, plant porn and more! **244 pages $14**

BB-005 **"Razor Wire Pubic Hair" Carlton Mellick III** — A genderless humandildo is purchased by a razor dominatrix and brought into her nightmarish world of bizarre sex and mutilation. **176 pages $11**

BB-006 **"Stranger on the Loose" D. Harlan Wilson** — The fiction of Wilson's 2nd collection is planted in the soil of normalcy, but what grows out of that soil is a dark, witty, otherworldly jungle... **228 pages $14**

BB-007 **"The Baby Jesus Butt Plug" Carlton Mellick III** — Using clones of the Baby Jesus for anal sex will be the hip sex fetish of the future. **92 pages $10**

BB-008 **"Fishyfleshed" Carlton Mellick III** — The world of the past is an illogical flatland lacking in dimension and color, a sick-scape of crispy squid people wandering the desert for no apparent reason. **260 pages $14**

BB-009 "Dead Bitch Army" Andre Duza — Step into a world filled with racist teenagers, cannibals, 100 warped Uncle Sams, automobiles with razor-sharp teeth, living graffiti, and a pissed-off zombie bitch out for revenge. **344 pages $16**

BB-010 "The Menstruating Mall" Carlton Mellick III — "The Breakfast Club meets Chopping Mall as directed by David Lynch." - Brian Keene **212 pages $12**

BB-011 "Angel Dust Apocalypse" Jeremy Robert Johnson — Meth-heads, man-made monsters, and murderous Neo-Nazis. "Seriously amazing short stories..." - Chuck Palahniuk, author of Fight Club **184 pages $11**

BB-012 "Ocean of Lard" Kevin L Donihe / Carlton Mellick III — A parody of those old Choose Your Own Adventure kid's books about some very odd pirates sailing on a sea made of animal fat. **176 pages $12**

BB-015 "Foop!" Chris Genoa — Strange happenings are going on at Dactyl, Inc, the world's first and only time travel tourism company.
"A surreal pie in the face!" - Christopher Moore **300 pages $14**

BB-020 "Punk Land" Carlton Mellick III — In the punk version of Heaven, the anarchist utopia is threatened by corporate fascism and only Goblin, Mortician's sperm, and a blue-mohawked female assassin named Shark Girl can stop them. **284 pages $15**

BB-027 "Siren Promised" Jeremy Robert Johnson & Alan M Clark — Nominated for the Bram Stoker Award. A potent mix of bad drugs, bad dreams, brutal bad guys, and surreal/incredible art by Alan M. Clark. **190 pages $13**

BB-031"Sea of the Patchwork Cats" Carlton Mellick III — A quiet dreamlike tale set in the ashes of the human race. For Mellick enthusiasts who also adore The Twilight Zone. **112 pages $10**

BB-032 **"Extinction Journals" Jeremy Robert Johnson** — An uncanny voyage across a newly nuclear America where one man must confront the problems associated with loneliness, insane dieties, radiation, love, and an ever-evolving cockroach suit with a mind of its own. **104 pages $10**

BB-037 **"The Haunted Vagina" Carlton Mellick III** — It's difficult to love a woman whose vagina is a gateway to the world of the dead. **132 pages $10**

BB-043 **"War Slut" Carlton Mellick III** — Part "1984," part "Waiting for Godot," and part action horror video game adaptation of John Carpenter's "The Thing." **116 pages $10**

BB-047 **"Sausagey Santa" Carlton Mellick III** — A bizarro Christmas tale featuring Santa as a piratey mutant with a body made of sausages. 124 pages $10

BB-048 **"Misadventures in a Thumbnail Universe" Vincent Sakowski** — Dive deep into the surreal and satirical realms of neo-classical Blender Fiction, filled with television shoes and flesh-filled skies. **120 pages $10**

BB-053 **"Ballad of a Slow Poisoner" Andrew Goldfarb** — Millford Mutterwurst sat down on a Tuesday to take his afternoon tea, and made the unpleasant discovery that his elbows were becoming flatter. **128 pages $10**

BB-055 **"Help! A Bear is Eating Me" Mykle Hansen** — The bizarro, heartwarming, magical tale of poor planning, hubris and severe blood loss...
150 pages $11

BB-056 **"Piecemeal June" Jordan Krall** — A man falls in love with a living sex doll, but with love comes danger when her creator comes after her with crab-squid assassins. **90 pages $9**

BB-058 "The Overwhelming Urge" Andersen Prunty — A collection of bizarro tales by Andersen Prunty. **150 pages $11**

BB-059 "Adolf in Wonderland" Carlton Mellick III — A dreamlike adventure that takes a young descendant of Adolf Hitler's design and sends him down the rabbit hole into a world of imperfection and disorder. **180 pages $11**

BB-061 "Ultra Fuckers" Carlton Mellick III — Absurdist suburban horror about a couple who enter an upper middle class gated community but can't find their way out. **108 pages $9**

BB-062 "House of Houses" Kevin L. Donihe — An odd man wants to marry his house. Unfortunately, all of the houses in the world collapse at the same time in the Great House Holocaust. Now he must travel to House Heaven to find his departed fiancee. **172 pages $11**

BB-064 "Squid Pulp Blues" Jordan Krall — In these three bizarro-noir novellas, the reader is thrown into a world of murderers, drugs made from squid parts, deformed gun-toting veterans, and a mischievous apocalyptic donkey. **204 pages $12**

BB-065 "Jack and Mr. Grin" Andersen Prunty — "When Mr. Grin calls you can hear a smile in his voice. Not a warm and friendly smile, but the kind that seizes your spine in fear. You don't need to pay your phone bill to hear it. That smile is in every line of Prunty's prose." - Tom Bradley. **208 pages $12**

BB-066 "Cybernetrix" Carlton Mellick III — What would you do if your normal everyday world was slowly mutating into the video game world from Tron? **212 pages $12**

BB-072 "Zerostrata" Andersen Prunty — Hansel Nothing lives in a tree house, suffers from memory loss, has a very eccentric family, and falls in love with a woman who runs naked through the woods every night. **144 pages $11**

BB-073 **"The Egg Man" Carlton Mellick III** — It is a world where humans reproduce like insects. Children are the property of corporations, and having an enormous ten-foot brain implanted into your skull is a grotesque sexual fetish. Mellick's industrial urban dystopia is one of his darkest and grittiest to date. **184 pages $11**

BB-074 **"Shark Hunting in Paradise Garden" Cameron Pierce** — A group of strange humanoid religious fanatics travel back in time to the Garden of Eden to discover it is invested with hundreds of giant flying maneating sharks. **150 pages $10**

BB-075 **"Apeshit" Carlton Mellick III** - Friday the 13th meets Visitor Q. Six hipster teens go to a cabin in the woods inhabited by a deformed killer. An incredibly fucked-up parody of B-horror movies with a bizarro slant. **192 pages $12**

BB-076 **"Fuckers of Everything on the Crazy Shitting Planet of the Vomit At smosphere" Mykle Hansen** - Three bizarro satires. Monster Cocks, Journey to the Center of Agnes Cuddlebottom, and Crazy Shitting Planet. **228 pages $12**

BB-077 **"The Kissing Bug" Daniel Scott Buck** — In the tradition of Roald Dahl, Tim Burton, and Edward Gorey, comes this bizarro anti-war children's story about a bohemian conenose kissing bug who falls in love with a human woman. **116 pages $10**

BB-078 **"MachoPoni" Lotus Rose** — It's My Little Pony... *Bizarro* style! A long time ago Poniworld was split in two. On one side of the Jagged Line is the Pastel Kingdom, a magical land of music, parties, and positivity. On the other side of the Jagged Line is Dark Kingdom inhabited by an army of undead ponies. **148 pages $11**

BB-079 **"The Faggiest Vampire" Carlton Mellick III** — A Roald Dahl-esque children's story about two faggy vampires who partake in a mustache competition to find out which one is truly the faggiest. **104 pages $10**

BB-080 **"Sky Tongues" Gina Ranalli** — The autobiography of Sky Tongues, the biracial hermaphrodite actress with tongues for fingers. Follow her strange life story as she rises from freak to fame. **204 pages $12**

BB-081 **"Washer Mouth" Kevin L. Donihe** - A washing machine becomes human and pursues his dream of meeting his favorite soap opera star. **244 pages $11**

BB-082 **"Shatnerquake" Jeff Burk** - All of the characters ever played by William Shatner are suddenly sucked into our world. Their mission: hunt down and destroy the real William Shatner. **100 pages $10**

BB-083 **"The Cannibals of Candyland" Carlton Mellick III** - There exists a race of cannibals that are made of candy. They live in an underground world made out of candy. One man has dedicated his life to killing them all. **170 pages $11**

BB-084 **"Slub Glub in the Weird World of the Weeping Willows"** **Andrew Goldfarb** - The charming tale of a blue glob named Slub Glub who helps the weeping willows whose tears are flooding the earth. There are also hyenas, ghosts, and a voodoo priest **100 pages $10**

BB-085 **"Super Fetus" Adam Pepper** - Try to abort this fetus and he'll kick your ass! **104 pages $10**

BB-086 **"Fistful of Feet" Jordan Krall** - A bizarro tribute to spaghetti westerns, featuring Cthulhu-worshipping Indians, a woman with four feet, a crazed gunman who is obsessed with sucking on candy, Syphilis-ridden mutants, sexually transmitted tattoos, and a house devoted to the freakiest fetishes. **228 pages $12**

BB-087 **"Ass Goblins of Auschwitz" Cameron Pierce** - It's Monty Python meets Nazi exploitation in a surreal nightmare as can only be imagined by Bizarro author Cameron Pierce. **104 pages $10**

BB-088 **"Silent Weapons for Quiet Wars" Cody Goodfellow** - "This is high-end psychological surrealist horror meets bottom-feeding low-life crime in a techno-thrilling science fiction world full of Lovecraft and magic..." -John Skipp **212 pages $12**

BB-089 "Warrior Wolf Women of the Wasteland" Carlton Mellick III
— Road Warrior Werewolves versus McDonaldland Mutants...post-apocalyptic fiction has never been quite like this. **316 pages $13**

BB-091 "Super Giant Monster Time" Jeff Burk — A tribute to choose your own adventures and Godzilla movies. Will you escape the giant monsters that are rampaging the fuck out of your city and shit? Or will you join the mob of alien-controlled punk rockers causing chaos in the streets? What happens next depends on you. **188 pages $12**

BB-092 "Perfect Union" Cody Goodfellow — "Cronenberg's THE FLY on a grand scale: human/insect gene-spliced body horror, where the human hive politics are as shocking as the gore." -John Skipp. **272 pages $13**

BB-093 "Sunset with a Beard" Carlton Mellick III — 14 stories of surreal science fiction. **200 pages $12**

BB-094 "My Fake War" Andersen Prunty — The absurd tale of an unlikely soldier forced to fight a war that, quite possibly, does not exist. It's Rambo meets Waiting for Godot in this subversive satire of American values and the scope of the human imagination. **128 pages $11**

BB-095 "Lost in Cat Brain Land" Cameron Pierce — Sad stories from a surreal world. A fascist mustache, the ghost of Franz Kafka, a desert inside a dead cat. Primordial entities mourn the death of their child. The desperate serve tea to mysterious creatures. A hopeless romantic falls in love with a pterodactyl. And much more. **152 pages $11**

BB-096 "The Kobold Wizard's Dildo of Enlightenment +2" Carlton Mellick III — A Dungeons and Dragons parody about a group of people who learn they are only made up characters in an AD&D campaign and must find a way to resist their nerdy teenaged players and retarded dungeon master in order to survive. 232 **pages $12**

BB-098 "A Hundred Horrible Sorrows of Ogner Stump" Andrew Goldfarb — Goldfarb's acclaimed comic series. A magical and weird journey into the horrors of everyday life. **164 pages $11**

BB-099 **"Pickled Apocalypse of Pancake Island" Cameron Pierce**—A demented fairy tale about a pickle, a pancake, and the apocalypse. **102 pages $8**

BB-100 **"Slag Attack" Andersen Prunty**— Slag Attack features four visceral, noir stories about the living, crawling apocalypse.A slag is what survivors are calling the slug-like maggots raining from the sky, burrowing inside people, and hollowing out their flesh and their sanity. **148 pages $11**

BB-101 **"Slaughterhouse High" Robert Devereaux**—A place where schools are built with secret passageways, rebellious teens get zippers installed in their mouths and genitals, and once a year, on that special night, one couple is slaughtered and the bits of their bodies are kept as souvenirs. **304 pages $13**

BB-102 **"The Emerald Burrito of Oz" John Skipp & Marc Levinthal** —OZ IS REAL! Magic is real! The gate is really in Kansas! And America is finally allowing Earth tourists to visit this weird-ass, mysterious land. But when Gene of Los Angeles heads off for summer vacation in the Emerald City, little does he know that a war is brewing...a war that could destroy both worlds. **280 pages $13**

BB-103 **"The Vegan Revolution... with Zombies" David Agranoff** — When there's no more meat in hell, the vegans will walk the earth. **160 pages $11**

BB-104 **"The Flappy Parts" Kevin L Donihe**—Poems about bunnies, LSD, and police abuse. You know, things that matter. 132 **pages $11**

BB-105 **"Sorry I Ruined Your Orgy" Bradley Sands**—Bizarro humorist Bradley Sands returns with one of the strangest, most hilarious collections of the year. **130 pages $11**

BB-106 **"Mr. Magic Realism" Bruce Taylor**—Like Golden Age science fiction comics written by Freud, *Mr. Magic Realism* is a strange, insightful adventure that spans the furthest reaches of the galaxy, exploring the hidden caverns in the hearts and minds of men, women, aliens, and biomechanical cats. **152 pages $11**

BB-107 **"Zombies and Shit" Carlton Mellick III**—"Battle Royale" meets "Return of the Living Dead." Mellick's bizarro tribute to the zombie genre. **308 pages $13**

BB-108 **"The Cannibal's Guide to Ethical Living" Mykle Hansen**— Over a five star French meal of fine wine, organic vegetables and human flesh, a lunatic delivers a witty, chilling, disturbingly sane argument in favor of eating the rich.. **184 pages $11**

BB-109 **"Starfish Girl" Athena Villaverde**—In a post-apocalyptic underwater dome society, a girl with a starfish growing from her head and an assassin with sea anenome hair are on the run from a gang of mutant fish men. **160 pages $11**

BB-110 **"Lick Your Neighbor" Chris Genoa**—Mutant ninjas, a talking whale, kung fu masters, maniacal pilgrims, and an alcoholic clown populate Chris Genoa's surreal, darkly comical and unnerving reimagining of the first Thanksgiving. **303 pages $13**

BB-111 **"Night of the Assholes" Kevin L. Donihe**—A plague of assholes is infecting the countryside. Normal everyday people are transforming into jerks, snobs, dicks, and douchebags. And they all have only one purpose: to make your life a living hell.. **192 pages $11**

BB-112 **"Jimmy Plush, Teddy Bear Detective" Garrett Cook**—Hardboiled cases of a private detective trapped within a teddy bear body. **180 pages $11**

BB-113 **"The Deadheart Shelters" Forrest Armstrong**—The hip hop lovechild of William Burroughs and Dali... **144 pages $11**

BB-114 **"Eyeballs Growing All Over Me... Again" Tony Raugh**—Absurd, surreal, playful, dream-like, whimsical, and a lot of fun to read. **144 pages $11**

BB-115 **"Whargoul" Dave Brockie** — From the killing grounds of Stalingrad to the death camps of the holocaust. From torture chambers in Iraq to race riots in the United States, the Whargoul was there, killing and raping. **244 pages $12**

BB-116 **"By the Time We Leave Here, We'll Be Friends" J. David Osborne** — A David Lynchian nightmare set in a Russian gulag, where its prisoners, guards, traitors, soldiers, lovers, and demons fight for survival and their own rapidly deteriorating humanity. **168 pages $11**

BB-117 **"Christmas on Crack" edited by Carlton Mellick III** — Perverted Christmas Tales for the whole family! . . . as long as every member of your family is over the age of 18. **168 pages $11**

BB-118 **"Crab Town" Carlton Mellick III** — Radiation fetishists, balloon people, mutant crabs, sail-bike road warriors, and a love affair between a woman and an H-Bomb. This is one mean asshole of a city. Welcome to Crab Town. **100 pages $8**

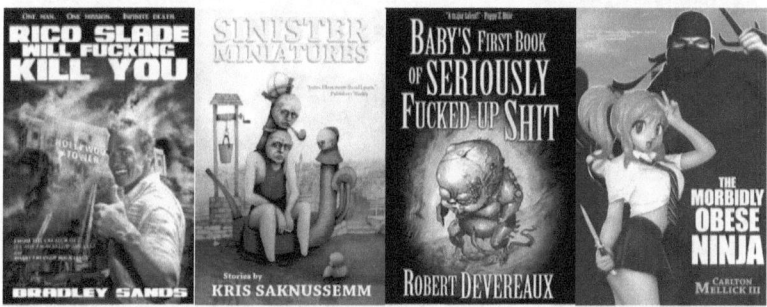

BB-119 **"Rico Slade Will Fucking Kill You" Bradley Sands** — Rico Slade is an action hero. Rico Slade can rip out a throat with his bare hands. Rico Slade's favorite food is the honey-roasted peanut. Rico Slade will fucking kill everyone. A novel. **122 pages $8**

BB-120 **"Sinister Miniatures" Kris Saknussemm** — The definitive collection of short fiction by Kris Saknussemm, confirming that he is one of the best, most daring writers of the weird to emerge in the twenty-first century. **180 pages $11**

BB-121 **"Baby's First Book of Seriously Fucked up Shit" Robert Devereaux** — Ten stories of the strange, the gross, and the just plain fucked up from one of the most original voices in horror. **176 pages $11**

BB-122 **"The Morbidly Obese Ninja" Carlton Mellick III** — These days, if you want to run a successful company . . . you're going to need a lot of ninjas. **92 pages $8**

BB-123 **"Abortion Arcade" Cameron Pierce** — An intoxicating blend of body horror and midnight movie madness, reminiscent of early David Lynch and the splatterpunks at their most sublime. **172 pages $11**

BB-124 **"Black Hole Blues" Patrick Wensink** — A hilarious double helix of country music and physics. **196 pages $11**

BB-125 **"Barbarian Beast Bitches of the Badlands" Carlton Mellick III** — Three prequels and sequels to *Warrior Wolf Women of the Wasteland*. **284 pages $13**

BB-126 **"The Traveling Dildo Salesman" Kevin L. Donihe** — A nightmare comedy about destiny, faith, and sex toys. Also featuring Donihe's most lurid and infamous short stories: *Milky Agitation, Two-Way Santa, The Helen Mower, Living Room Zombies,* and *Revenge of the Living Masturbation Rag.* **108 pages $8**

BB-127 **"Metamorphosis Blues" Bruce Taylor** — Enter a land of love beasts, intergalactic cowboys, and rock 'n roll. A land where Sears Catalogs are doorways to insanity and men keep mysterious black boxes. Welcome to the monstrous mind of Mr. Magic Realism. **136 pages $11**

BB-128 **"The Driver's Guide to Hitting Pedestrians" Andersen Prunty** — A pocket guide to the twenty-three most painful things in life, written by the most well-adjusted man in the universe. **108 pages $8**

BB-129 **"Island of the Super People" Kevin Shamel** — Four students and their anthropology professor journey to a remote island to study its indigenous population. But this is no ordinary native culture. They're super heroes and villains with flesh costumes and outlandish abilities like self-detonation, musical eyelashes, and microwave hands. **194 pages $11**

BB-130 **"Fantastic Orgy" Carlton Mellick III** — Shark Sex, mutant cats, and strange sexually transmitted diseases. Featuring the stories: *Candy-coated, Ear Cat, Fantastic Orgy, City Hobgoblins,* and *Porno in August.* **136 pages $9**

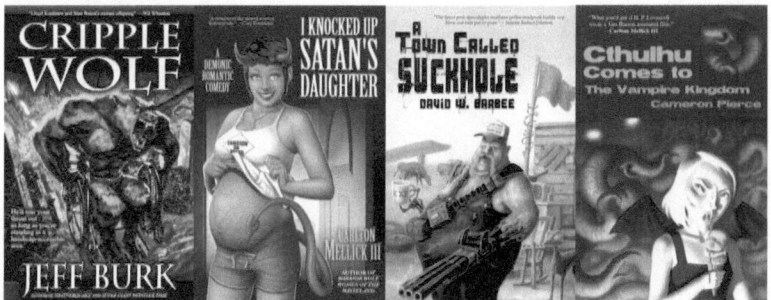

BB-131 **"Cripple Wolf" Jeff Burk** — Part man. Part wolf. 100% crippled. Also including *Punk Rock Nursing Home, Adrift with Space Badgers, Cook for Your Life, Just Another Day in the Park, Frosty and the Full Monty*, and *House of Cats*. **152 pages $10**

BB-132 **"I Knocked Up Satan's Daughter" Carlton Mellick III** — An adorable, violent, fantastical love story. A romantic comedy for the bizarro fiction reader. **152 pages $10**

BB-133 **"A Town Called Suckhole" David W. Barbee** — Far into the future, in the nuclear bowels of post-apocalyptic Dixie, there is a town. A town of derelict mobile homes, ancient junk, and mutant wildlife. A town of slack jawed rednecks who bask in the splendors of moonshine and mud boggin'. A town dedicated to the bloody and demented legacy of the Old South. A town called Suckhole. **144 pages $10**

BB-134 **"Cthulhu Comes to the Vampire Kingdom" Cameron Pierce** — What you'd get if H. P. Lovecraft wrote a Tim Burton animated film. **148 pages $11**

BB-135 **"I am Genghis Cum" Violet LeVoit** — From the savage Arctic tundra to post-partum mutations to your missing daughter's unmarked grave, join visionary madwoman Violet LeVoit in this non-stop eight-story onslaught of full-tilt Bizarro punk lit thrills. **124 pages $9**

BB-136 **"Haunt" Laura Lee Bahr** — A tripping-balls Los Angeles noir, where a mysterious dame drags you through a time-warping Bizarro hall of mirrors. **316 pages $13**

BB-137 **"Amazing Stories of the Flying Spaghetti Monster" edited by Cameron Pierce** — Like an all-spaghetti evening of Adult Swim, the Flying Spaghetti Monster will show you the many realms of His Noodly Appendage. Learn of those who worship him and the lives he touches in distant, mysterious ways. **228 pages $12**

BB-138 **"Wave of Mutilation" Douglas Lain** — A dream-pop exploration of modern architecture and the American identity, *Wave of Mutilation* is a Zen finger trap for the 21st century. **100 pages $8**